MW01615336

WTF

THIEF FOR HIRE

BOOK ONE

MARC-ALLEN BARKER

WTF: Thief for Hire
Copyright © 2022 by Marc-Allen Barker
All rights reserved.
Second Edition: 2024

Hardcover ISBN: 978-2-9585848-3-2
Paperback ISBN: 978-2-9585848-1-8
E-book ISBN: ISBN 978-2-9585848-0-1

Cover and Formatting: Streetlight Graphics

No part of this book may be reproduced, scanned, or distributed in any printed or electronic form without permission. Please do not participate in or encourage piracy of copyrighted materials in violation of the author's rights. Thank you for respecting the hard work of this author.

This is a work of fiction. Names, characters, places, and incidents either are the product of the author's imagination or are used fictitiously, and any resemblance to locales, events, business establishments, or actual persons—living or dead—is entirely coincidental.

A special thank you to my wife & son. Without your love and support I wouldn't have been able to do this.

"Sometimes we kick the ones we love"

TABLE OF CONTENTS

CHAPTER ONE

STRIP CLUBS AND VILLAINS

WILLIAM TREVOR FRANCIS, FORMER PARA WITH THE 1ST RHP based in Tarbes, located deep in the Hautes-Pyrénées of Southern France, took one last drag of his Camel Wide cigarette before unceremoniously flicking the butt into the street. He verified that it had hit the puddle of water by the drainage grate he was aiming for, exhaled the blue tobacco smoke through his nostrils, and entered the Golden Girls strip club on the Potsdamer Strasse, a short fifteen-minute walk away from his hotel. Paying the overweight, and unattractive, Eastern European woman the 20 Euros entrance fee, he opened the second, heavily padded, black double-diamond stitched leather door into the main room and entered the seedy and dimly-lit pleasure palace.

Glancing around, he clocked an empty table front-and-center, and signaling to one of the waitresses, made his way over to his seat. He knew the Golden Girls strip club well, and usually paid it a visit along with a substantial amount of money whenever he was in town. He could, of course, afford the nicer, higher-end 'gentleman clubs' that Berlin had to offer, but instead appreciated the grit, grime, and pseudo glamour of the 'working mans' club. He knew what he wanted, and he knew where he was comfortable getting it. Why go to a fancier establishment just to get hosed? Besides, Tatiana was working tonight, and he was looking forward to seeing her again, hopefully, a lot more of her, before the night was over.

Making himself comfortable in the slightly tattered and torn red crush velvet upholstered booth—thank God he'd never come in here with a black light—he removed his smokes from his pocket, sparked up a ciggy, and signaled the waitress again. The young lady, probably in her late twenties with an ample bosom and beer belly to match sauntered, nonchalantly, over to him.

"Was kann ich Ihnen bringen?" she asked.

William Trevor Francis could speak German. He could actually speak a handful of languages reasonably well. But he wasn't in the mood. Not tonight.

"Johnnie Walker Black. Double. Rocks on the side. And a clean ashtray."

Another reason he liked the Golden Girls club. He could smoke there. Management always turned a blind eye. The rules it would appear did not apply to them and therefore did not apply to him. The waitress sauntered off, her fluorescent-pink spandex-covered bum wagging as she walked away. She returned, only minutes later with his glass of scotch, a second glass containing his ice, and a clean ashtray.

"Hier, bitte."

"Thank you," he said. "That's great."

Taking another puff of his cigarette, he plopped two ice cubes into his drink, gave the glass a quick swirl, and then took a long, slow, deliberate sip. He waited a split second for the initial bite to burn his inner cheeks, then swallowed, savoring the warmth of the amber fluid as it hit his empty stomach.

In spite of his tailored Gieves & Hawkes suit and French cuffed dress shirt, he looked like shit and felt even worse. Retirement didn't suit him, and no matter how expensive his attire, the fact remained that he looked like crap! As Ringo Starr from the Beatles is once allegedly quoted to have said "You can't polish a turd, but you *can* roll it in glitter". No amount of fine clothing, expensive accessories, or shiny bling-bling glitter would help here though. William, quite honestly, looked more than a little worse for wear.

William Trevor Francis was a 'thief for hire'. Correction. William Trevor Francis *had been* a thief for hire—and a damn good one at that. But now his world revolved around excessive drinking, cheap women, and poor gambling as opposed to the high-end worlds of fine art, classic cars, corporate espionage, and the thrill of the chase that, up until a year ago, he had been accustomed to! Damn, he was bored. Bored and drinking too much. Bored, drinking too much, and getting fat.

A year ago he had been commissioned to acquire—natural-ly without consent from the owner—a rare 250 GT California

Spyder that, at auction in Maranello earlier in the year, had gone to a private collector in Southern California. The job was simple enough. Steal it from the new owners' collection in Montecito and deliver it down to a shipping container in the San Pedro docks, South of Los Angeles. His line of work took him all over the world, and whenever possible, he opted to steal *from* criminals, *for* criminals as much as he could. Criminals tended not to call the authorities when they'd been robbed, and as his experience had taught him over the years, most criminals deserved what they got. What goes around comes around. C'est la vie. Karma's a bitch. You get what you deserve—blah, blah, blah—the scotch was beginning to take effect. His mind was starting to ramble.

The steal itself had gone well, as expected. But the confrontation and altercation that had ensued on West Pier D Street adjacent to the maritime dealer and warehouse had ended badly for him. The pickup men at the docks had tried to short-change him out of his remaining '50% on delivery' fee and subsequently an argument, quickly followed by gratuitous violence and gunfire, had kicked off.

William knew how to handle himself better than most. "Strike First. Strike Hard. No Mercy". The cult hit Cobra Kai motto that he had been watching in his hotel room the night before couldn't have been more apt. But his aggression and ruthlessness towards the other men had cost him dearly. Upon hearing gunfire, the port authorities and port security officers were on the scene in what had seemed only a matter of minutes, and he had only just managed to escape the area by the skin of his teeth with a bullet in his thigh. Not only had he been shot, but he was also short a quarter of a million dollars. A quarter of a million dollars that he was banking on to pay off his expenses and gambling debts back home.

The stunningly beautiful car that could have saved him had now been impounded by the Long Beach Harbor Patrol. He was screwed. Hurt and screwed. Time for a different career path. As Danny Glover's character famously said in the first Lethal Weapon movie, he was getting too old for this shit!

He took another sip of his drink, followed by a puff on his ciggy, and contemplated his life, and predicament some more.

"Zeig mir das Geld." The loud German voice emanating from the corner D.J. booth said, quickly followed by a grammatically incorrect "Show me your money."

Looks like the club's punters weren't digging deep enough into their pockets. The girls on stage were complaining about the lack of tips being thrown their way.

He grinned to himself. He loved this place. Sure it was a shit-hole, and a bit rough around the edges, but so was a lot of Berlin. That's what made it so special. It was real. Down to earth. Unashamedly 'on the fringe' and unapologetic in its behavior, and attitude towards the world. Just for goodness sake don't look too closely at the cracks or peel away at the thin veneer masking its dark and seedy underbelly, because if you did, Berlin would bitch-slap you quicker than you could say "Entschuldige. Falsches Loch!"

Tatiana, the 30-something stripper on stage with killer legs and a matching 'I'm going to take you for everything you've got' attitude approached him, snapping him out of his scotch-induced melancholy. She crouched down in front of him, her legs sensuously splayed, and whipped her fake, platinum blonde wig over her shoulders.

He smiled, pulled a 50 Euro note from his money clip, and placed it, gently but assuringly, into her G-string.

"Hello, stranger. How you been keeping?" he asked her.

"Better than you. Where the Hell you been?"

"Keeping out of trouble for a change," he smirked.

"I've missed you. I haven't seen you in ages."

"Well, how about we catch up later?" he asked her confidently.

Tatiana grinned. She was glad to see him again, but she also wanted to play it cool. She knew him well enough and knew he enjoyed the game as much as she did. She looked him up and down.

"I don't know. You look terrible."

William blew her a cheeky kiss. "Love you too."

Tatiana smiled, pretended to catch the kiss on her cheek, and continued to work the stage and pole, shaking and swirling, her long acrylic hair whipping and flailing against her toned and tanned body. He smiled again at her and placed a second 50 Euro note on the lip of the blue-beaded light stage. She returned as soon as she saw it.

"I'm fairly busy tonight, but I get off at two," she told him.

"Two works."

Tatiana leaned forward, deliberately pushing her bronzed

B-cups into his face as she picked up the Euro bill before working the stage and the other customers in the club with front
row seats. William laughed to himself. Ahh. The simple plea-
sures in life he thought. Who said money can't buy happiness?

––––––––––––

At the other end of the main dance room, walking
through the doors to the club, a man, Vinny, stopped and
surveyed the surroundings, and its clientele. Vinny was, like
William, also in his late 40s. However, unlike William, Vinny
looked decidedly untrustworthy. An air of 'don't mess with me
or I'll slit your throat' permeated from his deeply pitted and
scarred skin. The two men had both served in the same regiment, and having worked together in the past, knew each other
well. William's military skills included surveillance, reconnaissance, close combat, and marksmanship. Vinny's unique skills
revolved around procurement. No matter what you wanted or
needed, if you couldn't get it through the usual channels Vinny
was your go-to guy. On the books, off the books, no questions
asked, Vinny was your man.

CHAPTER TWO

IT'LL BE A VACATION

Spotting William, Vinny made his way over to the booth and sat himself down. He ran his fingers through his slicked-back greasy hair and cracked a dangerous smile across his pasty white face. The same female waitress, now noticing a new man at the table, came over and asked him what he wanted to drink. He casually gestured to William's glass.

"Give me the same as him. Make that two. And more ice."

The waitress nodded and left. William continued to ignore them both.

As Tatiana, once again, approached their end of the stage, Vinny removed a small stack of dirty bills from his inside jacket pocket, and waved a single 5 Euro note, tantalizingly in front of his nose. Sliding over to him, he slipped the five firmly between her open legs and licked his lips. Tatiana, understandably, was startled, embarrassed, and possibly even a little scared. William, now acknowledging him for the first time piped up.

"Show some manners mate. And quit being so bloody cheap!"

He took another sip of his drink, and then drained it. Moments later, the waitress returned with the second round of drinks for them both. Vinny took a long pull at his whisky, his eyes fixed on the girl on stage, and turned to William.

"You're a hard man to find. I must've hit up every club in town."

William studied him closely. A fire of anticipation and imminent dread burning in the pit of his stomach.

"And now you've found me."

He placed two fresh ice cubes into his new drink, took a long pull, and looked at Vinny with steely determination and defiance in his eyes before turning his attention back to a second girl on stage.

"You still retired? 'Cos if you are, it doesn't suit you. You look like shit." Vinny quipped.

William rolled his eyes in acknowledgment and agreement. Hard to argue that one!

"What do you want, Vinny?" An air of exasperation clearly detectable in his voice.

"I got another job for you. Corporate gig this time. Some high-end pharma lab. Simple smash and grab type of deal. Get in, take the files, get out. Easy."

William gave a heavy sigh. He knew there would be an angle. Something that Vinny wanted, or expected from him.

"I'm not interested mate. I'm retired. You know that."

Vinny shuffled in his seat, inching closer, the inevitable car salesman pitch that was about to follow building inside of him.

"It's a quarter of a mill. Half in advance, half on completion, minus a small cut for me. Of course, you're interested. Who wouldn't be?"

Silence fell on the table like an anvil.

"What part of 'I'm retired' don't you get? I told you, I'm done. I don't need this anymore. Corporate gig or otherwise."

Annoyed with the conversation, and the fact that his evening was in the midst of being shot to Hell, William took another big gulp of his scotch.

"Anyway, I'm not interested in robbing a bloody pharmacy."

Vinny sighed heavily. He knew all too well that his old army pal could be a bloody stubborn bastard, but he was going to give it another shot. He had to. The job was simply too good to pass up. It was a silver-platter deal. A unicorn. A cash cow.

"Christ Almighty! For a quarter of a million will you at least consider it?" he pleaded.

William took a drag of his cigarette, stubbed it out in the ashtray, and let him hang, eyes fixed on the dancer in front of him, deep in thought.

"It's an easy job Will, especially for someone like you. Take the money. The job's in Budapest. You love that place. It'll be a vacation. Then you can drink and get fat and tip as many titty girls as you want. I won't ever bother you again. I promise!"

William took his time, internally mulling over his options. Since the debacle a year ago with the Ferrari, the loss of money, getting shot, and the stain on his reputation for not delivering the goods, things had definitely gone South for him. He knew very well that nothing that went wrong that night had been his fault. On the contrary, he had researched, planned, and executed his robbery according to plan incredibly well—as was expected for someone of his caliber and reputation. The fact that the tables had been turned on him when delivering the car had not been his fault. He was owed a remaining balance upon delivery at the port, and the fact that his counterparts were unwilling to pay up had started the long and unfortunate sequence of events forcing him underground, ultimately leading him to Berlin to lie low, rest, and recover. Later that night, in a quiet back room at the Golden Girls strip club, he was certain that he would win back his money in another private poker game, and hopefully minimize his debts. He was counting on it and had even dressed up for the part.

William Trevor Francis might have been a good-looking son of a bitch, and he may well have been an excellent thief. Possibly the best thief no one knew about. But he was also a shockingly bad gambler, and all too often, lost way more than he could afford to lose at the tables. Invariably, his heavy losses would then result in him taking on another 'custom robbery' to pay off his debts. He was good at what he did but, by God, he was his own worst enemy!

"Come on. You know you miss it," Vinny added out of desperation.

William turned his head, and looked Vinny dead in the eyes, before turning away again to focus his attention on the semi-nude, gyrating females in front of him. He turned back to Vinny.

"Let me mull it over and I'll let you know. No promises."

Deep down he already knew he didn't *want* the job, and if he won tonight he wouldn't *need* the job. But Vinny was an old mate and their loyalties to each other ran deep. The least he could do was let him down gently.

"That's what I'm talking about!"

Vinny, now satisfied and with his objective for the evening accomplished, threw down 80 Euros onto the table to cover the drinks, and slowly stood up.

"Retired my ass," he exclaimed. "And next time you're in town, spend your money at *my* joint will you. You've been hitting up every strip club in Berlin except mine. The girls are gonna start taking it personally."

William grinned, and then laughed aloud.

"It's not your girls I'm avoiding Vinny. It's you, you wanker!"

Vinny smirked back at him, the both of them aware that this job would be mutually beneficial. Both would come out on top. Vinny flipped him the bird.

"Once an asshole …" he said

"… always an asshole!" responded William.

With that, Vinny gave him a reassuring pat on the shoulder and walked away leaving William, once again, to his scotch, smokes, and strippers.

William Trevor Francis looked at the large luminescent hour markers of his Rolex Deepsea. It was just gone 8 pm. He pulled out two hundred Euro bills from his wallet and nodded over to Tatiana one last time to get her attention. She danced over to him picking up other scattered bills from the dance floor along her way. He gently placed the two bills in her hand.

"Apologies for my friend. He's a bit rough around the edges."

"That's OK. I'm used to it. We still on for later?" She batted her eyes enticingly.

"Of course. I'm just going to play a few hands around back. I'll pick you up by the side entrance at two."

She blew him a kiss affectionately.

"Thanks, hun'."

Satisfied, he got up, necked the remnants of his glass, grabbed his smokes, stuffed his pockets, and winked at her.

"Catch you later."

"Kisses," she said.

With that, he left the club floor and proceeded along the dark back corridor, behind the stage, and into the secluded room where the players for that evening's game were beginning to congregate.

LATER THAT EVENING, WILLIAM TREVOR FRANCIS FOUND himself seated at a table with four other players, a Kilimanjaro-sized pile of cash weighing heavily in its center. Cigarettes, cigars, bottles of clear, yellow, and brown liquor adorned the green felt-topped table. He contemplated the cards in his hand. He wasn't a great poker player, but he knew what he was doing and the table *had* to turn in his favor soon. He eyed the competition again, hesitated a split second, and pushed his remaining chips into the center stack.

"All in."

There was a gentle gasp and murmur of astonishment from around the table. The player to his left, a skinny, weasel-faced Romanian in his 50's with two gold front teeth, and a matching gold link necklace spoke first.

"I'm out," he said. The contempt in his voice as thick as the chain around his neck.

"Me too," said player three, a giant of a man called Sjard who operated a junk and scrap metal yard on the outskirts of Hamburg.

Player four, a usually cheerful, bald, and exuberant Bavarian pawn shop owner called Andreas was next.

"Fold," he said. "Sohn einer Hündin!"

Now, only player five, a decidedly dodgy German auto dealer from Munich called Pharis remained. Pharis studied the cards in his hand again, glanced up at his opponent, and then back down at his cards. He looked a second, and a third time, at the veritable fortune in front of him. A mega mountain of chips, Euros, Sterling, and Dollar bills. One of them was going to be a *very rich* individual at the end of all of this. Pharis eyed his cards one last time, puffed on his Cohiba Robusto, pondered, and then threw in his remaining chips.

"Call", he muttered.

William needed this win. He needed it badly. He estimated there was approximately one hundred thousand, possibly one-twenty on the table. Enough for him to pay off a significant portion of his debt. Not all of it, but enough. The table gasped and held its breath in eager anticipation as William flipped over his cards onto the tabletop. A Full House. He felt good. He felt like a winner.

Pharis nodded and eyed the cards in front of him, letting him hang for what seemed like an eternity.

"Four of a kind," Pharis said finally, as he laid out his four Kings and a seven of diamonds.

The table erupted.

"Bollocks!"

William Trevor Francis had lost everything. Gutted beyond belief, he got up, knocked back the last of his drink in one large gulp, lit another cigarette, and composed himself.

"Gentlemen, I'd like to tell you it's been a pleasure but that would be a bloody lie!"

Pharis, scooping his winnings over to his side of the felt, let out a hearty 'it's good to be me' belly laugh.

"The pleasure was all mine my friend!" he said, grinning ear to ear with delight at his dejected opponent.

Andreas chimed in, baffled, and confused. "Was Zur Hölle? What did you think you were doing?"

William shrugged. What else could he do? He'd lost fair and square. Now he had no option but to take it on the chin like a man, hold his head up high, and hope to win it all back the next time.

"Easy come easy go gentlemen. Now, if you don't mind, I have a beautiful young lady waiting for me who requires my attention and whatever money I've got left, for the evening."

The table chuckled. They liked this Englishman. Dependable, true to his word, and professional. If he owed you money he'd either steal something you wanted or pay you off when his next big job came along. He was a good loser.

William gathered his belongings, thanked the table for their hospitality, and exited the room. Walking down the corridor and back into the main hall he took out his cellphone and called Vinny.

"Lady Luck just screwed me over. Looks like I'm going to take that job after all. I'll get the details from you tomorrow."

With that, he hung up, exited the club, and turned the corner to wait for Tatiana who, he hoped, would at least offer him some small consolation for the evening.

CHAPTER THREE

NICE TO MEET YOU MARIE

THE NEXT WEEK, HAVING MET UP WITH VINNY TO AC-quire and discuss the necessary details, and equipment needed, William Trevor Francis, sporting dark glasses, a black leather jacket, blue jeans and biker boots emerged from the Budapest Ferenc Liszt International Airport terminal with his suitcase, suiter, and duffel bags in hand. A beautiful woman crossed his path causing him to rubber-neck, and take a good long hard look. European women were just so damn sexy. Even when they didn't try. Particularly when they didn't care. No matter what size, shape, or age they just oozed sexiness, and class. *Yes, that was the right word* he thought to himself, *Class.* The way they carried themselves, the way they conducted and composed themselves. It was unparalleled.

He pulled out his packet of smokes, sparked up, and after a few deep draws made his way over to the corner curb, to one of the many waiting taxis in line. Opening the rear door, he threw his bags onto the back seat, extinguished his cigarette curbside, and climbed in.

"Ritz-Carlton. Chain Bridge," he told the driver.

The cabbie immediately pulled out into a barrage of honking horns, disappearing down the airport ring road, and out onto the exit ramp towards the city center, leaving a thick blue trail of diesel fumes in his wake.

BEHIND THE HOTEL CHECK-IN DESK AT THE RITZ-Carlton, Amie Zezulka, an attractive receptionist with a killer body, greeted him with an inviting smile and a warm demeanor.

"Welcome to The Ritz-Carlton. Do you have a reservation?" she asked.

"Yes. The name's Allen. Nicholas Allen".

William had a slew of fake names, passports, and credit cards in his possession. He was an expert when it came to covering his tracks, and as such had successfully been able to elude the authorities throughout the years. He also knew when he needed to lay low, especially if a high-profile heist he had carried out was garnering too much unwanted attention. He was a ghost, which made him all the more successful at his job.

"One moment sir," she continued, tapping away at her computer keyboard, her eyes fixed on the monitor in front of her.

William took a moment to gaze around the lobby area, to

properly take in his surroundings. It had been a couple of years since he had last been here. They must have recently done a renovation. *Looks good,* he thought to himself. He shifted his gaze back to the lovely receptionist, then to the various hotel guests milling around in the background.

"If I could please have a credit card and passport, Mr. Allen," she asked, finally finding and confirming his reservation in the system.

He smiled, removed his wallet, and handed her a credit card along with a passport, both under the name Nicholas Allen. Once verified, she swiped both and returned them to him.

"I show you here for one week. Is that correct?"

"For now," he replied.

"Suite 529 is all ready for you. If I can just get you to sign here."

She handed him his key card, room contract and a Ritz-Carlton branded pen to sign it with. Their fingers brushing, ever so lightly, in the process.

"Is there a particular paper you'd prefer in the morning?" she asked him.

"Only if you're going to deliver it." A warm smile and a wink followed, what he later acknowledged to himself, was an atrociously poor pick-up line.

She smiled and blushed.

"The porter will help you with your bags. Enjoy your stay, Mr. Allen."

"I'm sure I will. Thank you," he responded.

With that, he grabbed his affairs, handed his bags to the young blond-haired bellboy, and walked over to the main bank of elevators around the corner. Outside his room, the young bellboy set down the suitcase, duffel bags, and Tumi suiter on the floor and opened the heavy, eggshell white door.

William entered the room and nodded his head in approval.

"This doesn't suck does it?"

The bellboy chuckled.

"No, it doesn't, sir."

William strolled around the room, taking it all in, before making his way over to the large panoramic windows framing the majestic view of Chain Bridge and Castle Hill situated on the opposite Buda side of the Danube river. He observed the luxury river cruise ship moored on the rear dock and studied the jubilant and carefree passengers dining al fresco on the rooftop. *Must be nice* he thought. *One day!*

He continued to soak up the view like a sponge. *What a city.* Breathtaking in its beauty, architecture, and history. He loved Budapest. Loved it! Prague was another city he loved. It reminded him of Paris—or what he imagined Paris would have looked like 100 years ago—without the thousands of tourists on every bloody corner. Its Charles Bridge, spanning the Vltava river, with its Catholic statues connecting the Old Town with the Mala Strana and Castle was also a stunningly beautiful piece of architecture and design. *Maybe he'd lie low in Prague for a while once the job was done*, he mused to himself. He turned his attention back to the bellboy.

"Can you arrange for a bottle of Johnnie Walker to be sent up? Black Label. And plenty of ice."

"Yes sir. No problem."

Taking out a small wad of notes he slipped the bellboy a generous tip.

"Thanks. I appreciate it."

As the bellboy exited, he once again turned his focus and attention out the window. This time deep in thought about the job at hand. The purpose of this visit. His raison d'être.

Within an hour, he was sitting at his hotel room desk with his laptop open in front of him, a crystal tumbler of scotch by his side. Entering his password, and selecting the correct encrypted files, he typed in the second password requirement and then sat back, waiting and watching as the blue screen sprang to life and populated itself with building schematics, blueprints, employee i.d. badges, and photos of a few select employees with high-security clearance.

Analyzing the various photos, he finally found the one he was looking for. A head-to-waist shot of a woman, brunette, hair pulled back in her mid-50's. He clicked on her thumbnail and zoomed in on her name badge. MARIE BOYER Ph.D. Allied Laboratories Senior Research Analyst.

"Nice to meet you, Marie," he whispered under his breath to himself.

CHAPTER FOUR

AND THE BUILDING GOES 'BOOM'

FOUR DAYS LATER, UNDER A BRIGHT MORNING SUN, William Trevor Francis, coffee and egg McMuffin sandwich in hand, proceeded on foot along the Dózsa György main road. He was about a twenty-minute walk east of the dividing Danube river, in the city's sixth district, but still comfortably within the Hungária Körút ring road that encased the Pest half of Budapest.

Passing by the outskirts of the city's immaculate Városliget park with its 18th-century castle, lakes, museums, and thermal baths he made a left at Hero's Square, cut through the middle along the southern rim of the lake, and back down to the polished Ötvenhatosok Tere monument before doubling back on himself to the Kunsthalle Art Museum. If there was one thing he was good at, it was making sure he wasn't being followed.

Continuing along the park's perimeter, he crossed over to the main road, and sat himself down on a roadside bench, over-looking the smoke-mirrored and steel-clad façade of the Allied Laboratories facility opposite him.

Retrieving a bottle of pills from his leather coat pocket he promptly swallowed four of the small white oval codeine tablets, the piping hot coffee burning his esophagus in the process. Damn, his hangover was killing him. Too much booze. He should have taken the blasted pills *before* he went to bed last night—not now—he thought to himself, shaking his head at his own stupidity. Now he'd just have to suffer through in silence until the drugs kicked in.

Settling in, and hunkering down into his position, he start-ed watching and noting the arrival and departure times of the various laboratory employees, the location of the security guards outside, their checkpoints, the location and angles of the exterior cameras, and most importantly, the arrival times, departure times, procedural duties, and habits of the interior night-shift lobby guards, and personnel.

This was now his third visit to the building, and his second perimeter reconnaissance. He was feeling confident. The inte-rior schematics were detailed enough and he was sufficiently optimistic about the job at hand. *Perfect Planning Prevents Piss-Poor Performance* he mused to himself. His father had drilled the six-P's into him from a very young age. The army had reinforced it.

A security guard approached the Allied Laboratories facil-ity main gates, swiped his card, chatted briefly with the guard outside, and entered. William checked his watch once more and noted the time. Bang on schedule. Like clockwork.

Two pretty women in their early thirties, one a petite 5'4" short-haired pixie-cut blonde with an impressive DD chest, and the other a 5'8" long-haired brunette with a diamond stud nose ring, butterfly belly ring, and a full sleeve of ink strolled past him as he sat, mesmerized, on his park bench. He took a moment to check them both out, looking them both up and down, admiring their curves, their beauty, their confidence, and above all their fun, carefree attitude. From around the back of the bench, presumably having come from somewhere inside the park, a long-haired black and tan Alsatian dog paced up to him, sniffing at the sausage patty in his 'breakfast of champions'.

He smiled. He loved animals. All animals. Cats, dogs, horses—it didn't matter—he loved them all. Way more than people. Animals loved unconditionally once you earned their trust. There was never a hidden agenda, an ulterior motive, or a spiteful, hurtful intention behind an animal's behavior or affections. You simply had to put in the time and effort to look after them, to care for them properly, and they in return showed you unconditional amounts of affection and loyalty. Humans on the other hand were the polar opposite. Especially in his experience and in his line of work. In his book, there were three codes of conduct, three lines you never crossed. The abuse of women, children, or animals. Those were his three 'no go' areas. His three 'points of no return'. Cross one of those lines and he was never going to let you forget it. The world could be on fire, burning to Hell, but if you intentionally hurt or inflicted harm on a woman, child, or animal he'd hurt you back. In a heartbeat.

He patted the dog on its head, scratched around the back of its ears, and checked for a collar and tags. The dog had neither but was in good condition, seemed to know what it was doing and where it was going, so William wasn't overly concerned. Taking one last bite of his McMuffin, he gave the rest to the dog who devoured it in two quick bites. Content, and realizing there was no more food to be had, the dog spun around, sniffed at the park bench, and cocked its leg.

"What the Hell!" he exclaimed, chunks of masticated sausage, egg, and bread flying from his mouth. The dog, naturally, ignored him and, when finished, walked away. Dog 1. WTF 0.

William took another long sip of his coffee. The pills had finally kicked in and the jackhammer in his head had mercifully turned off. He checked his watch again and then turned his attention back to the Allied Laboratories facility.

Five minutes later, a second security guard exited the lab. *One shift over, another beginning*, he thought to himself. With that, he took out his phone, and holding it up in front of him as if trying to get better cell reception, took another batch of perimeter and personnel photos.

Moments later, a large Aldi lorry passed in front of him. In the split second that his view of the building opposite had been blocked, he had disappeared from his scouting position leaving both the bench and the sidewalk empty, save the two pretty young women who were now conversing enthusiastically at the bottom of the road.

Further down the street, parked opposite the women, and with a clear view of where William had been sitting just moments earlier, a man in a blacked-out Jaguar put down his camera and started his car. He pulled out into the road, pumped the gas, and roared up the street, past the laboratory, before disappearing into heavy traffic around the corner.

———————

TWO DAYS LATER WILLIAM TREVOR FRANCIS WAS BACK IN his hotel room, and back at his desk, his two laptop screens open in front of him. The first, with the blueprints to the Allied Laboratories building, the second displaying a 'download 98% complete' bar. Strewn across his desk, papers, charts, diagrams, and blank key cards blocked out the desk's dark brown lacquered surface.

He eyed the monitors, heavy circles hanging like vintage drapery from his red, swollen, and bloodshot eyes. He had been preparing for the job, tirelessly, day and night for six days now. Planning was one thing, but he was methodical. Some would even say obsessive. Every turn, every possible scenario, every eventuality—no matter how small or unlikely—had to be considered. The Devil was *always* in the details.

Finally, with the laptop's internal fans kicking into overdrive, whining like a banshee, the download he was waiting for was finished. Clicking through the open tabs for the Allied Laboratories employee list, he selected and opened Marie Boyer's employee file, accessed her name badge, security clearance codes, and pressed ENTER.

The custom-written program that he had received in lieu of payment from a government cyber surveillance whistleblower a few years back had quickly become the most valuable tool in his toolbox. With his obsessive attention to detail—paired with the program's ability to penetrate *any* secure network—he had been able to hack countless 'impregnable' systems over the years. Verifying, once more, that her clearance pass would not only get him into the building but that it would also get him to where he needed to be, he grabbed the security card reader-writer device and swiped a blank magstripe employee i.d. badge through it. The laptop chugged away dutifully copying her security card data onto it.

Pleased with himself, he stretched and sighed heavily. Verifying photos of the nighttime security guards along with their 'start and end time' shifts, he got up from his chair and walked over to the bathroom. Staring at his tired, puffy-faced reflection in the mirror, he muttered *"Show Time"* to himself and turned on the sink faucets.

Thirty minutes later, he was showered, shaved, and dressed in his black slacks and dark blue crew neck sweater. Grabbing his belongings, he checked his equipment once more, double verified his devices, triple-checked his schematics, and turned down the lights to his room. It was just past midnight.

Outside the Allied Laboratories building, but this time from within the building grounds, William Trevor Francis—crouching in the dark shadows of the perfectly manicured shrubbery—pulled out a small pair of binoculars. He had originally thought about bringing his handheld ATN night vision goggles, but there was no point here as the main building atrium and lobby corridors were all fully lit up. His goggles would have served little to no purpose.

Two security guards, one of them with his boots up on the desk counter, sat idly watching the securing monitors in front of them. On one of the guard's phones, the first Mission Impossible movie was playing—its main character, Ethan Hunt—was dangling from a wire harness as he tried to hack into a high-security computer system safely locked away in a seemingly impenetrable vault.

William checked his watch. It was 2:15 am. *Should be anytime now* he thought to himself. Right on cue, the security guard with his feet on the counter plonked them down onto the floor and readjusted his trousers, crotch, and waistband. He grabbed his clipboard and sighed heavily. It was time to make his hourly rounds.

William's attention, his eyes having previously been leveled on the two security guards, was now transfixed on a third, previously unseen nighttime janitor in his late 50's. He hadn't registered him before and didn't know who he was, where he'd come from, or how long he had been there. It irked him. He didn't like surprises, especially ones that could compromise his work. He focused again, readjusted his binoculars, and followed the man who had now stepped out of the ground floor elevators, and who was slowly stowing his cleaning cart, mops, and trash bags into the downstairs cleaning cupboard.

He continued to watch him, like a hawk, until he exited the building and disappeared through the parking lot, and around the corner. *Only a janitor* he thought to himself, *nothing to worry about*. With his undivided attention back on the guard in the main lobby, he waited patiently for the right moment to strike. *Patience is a virtue. Patience is a virtue* he muttered to himself under his breath. Finally, as he had seen happen on the previous nights, the second security guard stood up from behind the main lobby counter and made his way over to the soft drinks vending machine.

Outside, William, seizing the moment, got to his feet and ran swiftly towards the main building, paying particular attention to the overhead cameras, and using the shadows to the best of his advantage. Removing his keycard and swiping the door pad he held his breath until he heard the tell-tale 'click' of the door bolt mechanism unlocking. Gently opening the door he let himself in.

Once inside, he darted over to the main desk. Hearing the sound of a soda bottle tumbling down through the drink dispenser and banging into the tray below, he scurried around the corner and down the brightly illuminated corridor, undetected. With the security guard now back in his chair, oblivious to the intrusion, William Trevor Francis hugged the wall, and raced down the corridor, avoiding the view of the security cameras, until he reached the stairwell.

Opening the door to the building's stairwell, he sprinted up the stairs stopping briefly on the fourth floor to catch his breath. *Damn, I'm out of shape!* he thought to himself. He checked his watch—and his pulse—and continued on. *Only two more flights to go*, he thought.

Once on the sixth floor, and forever mindful of the cameras, as well as the patrolling security guard who could be anywhere in the building, he edged his way down the hallway, stopping at a heavily smoked glass door. Racing against the clock, he removed his fake i.d. badge, embedded with Marie Boyer's high-security clearance access, and swiped the magnetic strip.

BOOM!

The laboratory doors exploded, fire and smoke engulfing the whole vicinity. Glass was blown everywhere as William was catapulted backwards into the hallway. Fire alarms erupted as the overhead sprinklers, simultaneously, began raining down upon him.

Barely conscious, he pulled himself along the wet, glass-ridden floor. Squinting into the main laboratory, now burning in its own rubble and ruin, he was able to make out the still, lifeless body of a dark-haired woman wearing a lab coat, her face barely visible in the wreckage. He recognized the face immediately. It belonged to Marie Boyer. A perfectly round bullet hole piercing the middle of her forehead.

His mind awash with confusion, he snapped himself back to reality, forbidding himself any semblance of reprieve, and got to his feet, unsteady and understandably shook up. The guards were coming.

What seemed like milliseconds later, the two security guards came crashing through the stairwell doors, with alarm bells ringing, wall lights flashing, sprinklers spouting, and sirens, audible in the distance, getting nearer by the second.

By the skin of his teeth, and undoubtedly aided by the

smoke, fire, and general mayhem, he managed to roll into a small alcove and hide, just in the nick of time, as the guards ran past him. Making his way back to the stairwell, with the two guards focused on the body of the dead woman, he stumbled back down the steps, holding his arms tight around his abdominal area which was now covered in blood.

The wailing of the emergency vehicles and the police sirens that were fast approaching was deafening, especially after an explosion. His ears were bleeding. He was doubled over in pain—cut, beaten, and bruised. But he was alive.

OUTSIDE IN THE CARPARK, WATCHING EVERYTHING FROM the safety and comfort of his black Jaguar, sat the janitor, Franz. A quiet, ruthless, and sadistic individual who had been following William Trevor Francis's every move since his arrival in Budapest. He cracked a smile, satisfied at the job he had carried out, a matte black Beretta 9mm with suppressor laying on the passenger seat beside him. Just as he was about to leave, Franz noticed the man in black, obviously wounded and in pain, limp out of the building, and disappear into the cold, dark night.

As the police cars, ambulances, and fire engines, all with their sirens blaring, arrived at the scene, Franz simultaneously started his engine and slowly pulled out of the rear of the car park, away from the commotion. Still sporting his tan-colored driving gloves, he removed the cell phone from his inside sports coat pocket and dialed.

"We've got a problem. He's still alive."

The line went dead.

CHAPTER FIVE

A STICKLER FOR THE RULES

MONIQUE LEFORT WAS IN A RUSH. WEARING HER DARK grey two-piece Givenchy suit, she tucked her files under her left arm, clamped her pen between her teeth, and pulled her long black silky hair into a tight, professional bun. With no hairpin available to her, she pulled the pen from her mouth and skewered her hair into place.

Monique, in her late 30's, was all business. She had joined Interpol's National Central Bureau in Paris three years ago and had spent the last two hours of her morning preparing a last-minute report for the eight DRI staff that were waiting for her in room 13A.

These officers specialized in specific crime areas, including organized crime, drugs, human trafficking, cybercrime, and high-end art theft. Monique Lefort, having been woken from her deep slumber by her superior, had summoned them all at short notice in response to a situation that had occurred in the early hours of that morning in Budapest. The unique working structure of the DRI in Paris enabled it to respond quickly, and comprehensively, to national law enforcement units that required international police cooperation to advance their investigations. This is what she excelled at. This is what her career path had been leading up to.

"Lieutenant," The voice of her boss, Capitaine Kristoff, caught her off guard.

She spun around to face him.

"Capitaine," she replied, with a heavy French accent.

"Good morning Lieutenant. I take it you've been fully briefed?"

"Yes, Capitaine. I've made all the necessary preparations. My team's waiting for me inside."

"I'm glad to hear it. This is a big one for you. You know that, right?"

"Yes, Capitaine. I've got this," she responded assertively.

"Good. Then don't leave your team waiting. Let me know how it goes."

"Yes, Capitaine. And thank you, again, for this opportunity."

Capitaine Kristoff had been the one who, upon hearing about the explosion and murder from the station's night officer, had called her. Monique had transferred to his division only a short while ago, but in that brief period of time, she had proven herself to be a valuable asset to the department and an intuitive team leader. This case, going by the initial details he had been given, had all the markings of a major criminal investigation, and if she could rally the troops, compile the dossier, apprehend the suspects and 'seal the deal' then it would be a major accomplishment for her, and a great feather in *his* cap.

He supported her devotion to her work and thought very highly of her skills, resourcefulness, and professional capabilities in an office environment, but he knew from personal experience that a high profile case like this—along with the attention and media scrutiny it was bound to garner—also had the potential to backfire big time. *Quel cauchemar! Rather her than me* he thought to himself before heading towards his own office and the relative safety therein.

Composing herself outside the conference room doors, she took a deep breath, double-checked her attire, exhaled, and marched in with her head held high. Confidence was key in her line of work, and Monique Lefort had a bigger set of balls than the biggest Alpha male in the room. It's what made her so damn formidable at her job. *'Lefort'. 'The Strong'.* This girl's bite really *was* worse than her bark.

Inside the room, the capable eight agents were already seated around the central glass-topped table, cups of freshly brewed black coffee, croissants, chocolatines, and pain aux raisin neatly laid out in front of them. They stiffened up as Monique walked in and took command of the room.

"Bonjour tout le monde," she said. "Thank you for coming at such short notice."

With that, she placed her files on the table in front of her and nodded to her deputy. The projector turned on, and simultaneously the main overhead conference room lights were turned down revealing an image of the burning building and a gaping hole on the sixth floor, where the laboratory—only hours earlier—used to be.

Monique made her way to the front of the room. Despite her 5'6" frame, she cut an impressive and imposing figure at the head of the table, her athletic, toned physique clearly visible through the delicate cloth of her attire. Whether it was yoga, pilates, or kettlebell training, whatever this woman was doing was working for her. She looked bloody great!

"At 0300 hours, we were briefed by our team in Budapest of a bombing at the Allied Laboratories, approximately 25 kilometers East of the Danube river. So far we have one reported victim. A fifty-four-year-old Head Research Scientist by the name of Marie Boyer who was shot in the head at close range."

She clicked the next slide. Everyone in the room was now giving her their undivided attention. The image of the murdered woman magnified on the screen in front of them. She grabbed the projector's clicker again and moved onto the next slide showing a picture of a man, sitting on a bench opposite the lab.

"This is our main person of interest."

As she continued to go through her presentation she clicked through various other nighttime and daytime photos of the man outside the lab. Looking at two passing women. Feeding a stray dog. Blowing smoke rings into the air, seemingly without a care in the world, and finally, an image of the same man limping through a back door of the burning Allied Laboratories building, having unknowingly been captured by CCTV in his haste to escape.

"William Trevor Francis," she continued, letting his name hang in the air a split second longer than was necessary.

"Mid to late '40s, 5'11", approximately 200 lbs, brown eyes, medium-length brown hair, British, ex-military, re-nowned thief to criminal gangs and private collectors. He's been in my sights for the last two years, but I've never been able to catch him or get him properly identified. Until now."

A male agent, in his late 20's, and wearing a cheap navy blue three-buttoned suit, piped up.

"What's his M.O?" he asked.

"As far as we can tell, money, women, and gambling," she responded.

"I think I like him," said a second male agent to his female colleague, who was clearly unimpressed by this behavior.

"Grow up!" she cut back.

Monique continued with her presentation, undeterred.

"William Trevor Francis is responsible for some of the biggest art heists to date. He's notoriously deceptive, blends in well, covers his tracks, and makes his living selling custom stolen pieces on the black market. Trust me, there's nothing to like about him!"

A gentle murmur filled the room.

"Why haven't we got him yet?" one of the other female

agents asked. Her obvious disdain for this 'WTF character' written all over her prematurely wrinkled and sunbed-burnt face.

"We simply haven't had the leads. There have been reports of him over the years in Athens, Vienna, and Los Angeles, but nothing concrete. Not until last night." She turned her attention back to the photo being projected on the screen and continued.

"We received an anonymous tip-off earlier this morning about his whereabouts, along with these photos. We're working as fast as we can to verify its credibility. I've sent you all his file. This man is our top priority."

Silence fell around the table as the agents continued with their breakfasts, eagerly digesting their pastries and this new information in equal measure. This was a lot to process, especially on an empty stomach.

"We *will* apprehend the suspect William Trevor Francis. Do I make myself clear?"

A short murmur shot around the room. No one dared put their head above the parapet and question her. They all knew better than that.

Lieutenant Monique Lefort had been slowly fighting her way up the chain of command since enrolling with the Gendarmerie Nationale straight out of University. Using her brains instead of brawn and her skills in lieu of looks, she had successfully and proficiently proven to her fellow colleagues that when it came to her role within Interpol's DRI Agency, she had earned her position. Young and brilliant, she was a stickler for the rules, for procedure, and for due diligence. While there was nothing strikingly beautiful about her physically, in the brains and talent department she was *smoking hot,* definitely a 10, and a force to be reckoned with.

CHAPTER SIX

AND THE TV WENT CRASH!

Back in his room, William Trevor Francis, beaten, bloodied, and battered, was seated at his desk, surfing the net trying to find some answers. He had managed to flee the burning building just as the authorities had descended onto the premises and had, for an hour or more, managed to slowly and carefully stagger back to his hotel room undetected. It had not been easy, and it had been an hour wrought with pain and anguish, but he had dug deep into his mental and physical reserves and had pulled through.

Now, back in the safety of his room, he was analyzing the finer details and smaller intricacies of the job. He was determined to figure out what the Hell had just happened. He got up, switched on the hotel room TV, and sitting on the edge of the bed, clicked through the channels until he got to an early morning local news station.

He sat bolt upright, mortified at what he was watching.

He read the red *Breaking News* ticker tape at the bottom of the screen.

"EXPLOSION AT ALLIED LABORATORIES IN BUDAPEST. LEAD SCIENTIST MURDERED IN BLAST"

Above the *Breaking News* footer, images of a blown-out and burning building filled the screen. Firemen were dumping water onto its white-hot embers, and billows of thick black toxic smoke were filling the air, obscuring the camera lenses. The scene could have come straight out of a Hollywood 'Yippee-ki-yay' blockbuster movie.

Panicked, he switched channels to an alternate news station.

"TERROR STRIKES AT ALLIED LAB EXPLOSION"

So much for a simple 'smash and grab' he thought to himself.

Rising gingerly from the bed, his cuts and wounds having been carefully cleaned and dressed—but still sore as Hell—he went back to his desk, and back to his computer.

Clicking on the employee i.d. photo of Marie Boyer, he sat back in his chair. None of this made any sense to him. He had done everything correctly. Everything he was supposed to have checked and carried out had been done methodically 'to a T'. Thinking back, the only unforeseen and unexpected question mark for him had been the janitor. He hadn't seen that one coming, and despite trying to convince himself otherwise, it hadn't rested easy with him. His initial instincts had told him something wasn't right, and over the years his instincts had never been wrong. He should have listened to them.

He looked back at the photo of Marie Boyer one more time and then, this time following his intuition, booted up the custom-made government surveillance software once more and hacked into the main INTERPOL server. He had needed to do this once before whilst hiding out in Athens a few years ago, but back then it had proven impossible. Since then, however, he had called in many favors and had learned, and acquired, the necessary skills and software patches for his current program. Now he was able to get what he wanted. It wasn't easy, but it *was* possible!

On the TV screen, clear as the patchy grey whiskers on his stubbled chin, was a photo of him sitting on the roadside bench from two days earlier. If he had been eating or drinking, the contents of his mouth would undeniably have been sprayed across the room. *WTF!? Who took these pictures?* he asked himself. *This can't be happening!*

Outside, five floors down and doing their best Fast & Furious impersonations, a fleet of police cars with their sirens blaring rocketed down the Erzsébet Tér main drag. Skidding to an abrupt halt outside the Ritz-Carlton main entrance, they blocked the outside valet parking areas and began setting up a defensive perimeter.

William, upon first hearing the sirens and then seeing the police cars descend on the hotel, was beside himself. *What the Hell?* he thought to himself. *This cannot be happening!*

What happened next was a blur. A Molotov cocktail of adrenaline, testosterone, and abject fear. As if on autopilot, he started to gather his belongings, manically stuffing his two laptops, phone, blueprints, and tactical gear into his bag.

Grabbing a pair of trousers and a sweater he hurriedly dressed, threw on a pair of shoes, and then, hearing the heavy drum of police boots stomping down the corridor, heaved a heavy wooden chest of draws in front of the door forming a barricade. This, he hoped, would buy him a few more precious seconds.

William was sweating and panting profusely. His heart was pounding. A man of his age couldn't possibly take much more of this. His day had gotten off to a horrific start, and he hadn't even had breakfast yet. *How much worse could this get?*

There was a loud banging at the door, followed by an equally loud and commanding order.

"Police! Open the door!" barked a voice from the other side.

The banging and shouting at the door continued as he grabbed the wooden desk chair and threw it with all his might against the window. It bounced back, a little worse for wear. The window had only cracked a little.

"Bollocks!" he exclaimed in frustration.

Wasting no time at all, he ripped the television set out of its wall-mount and frantically started to hammer it against the cracked glass, pounding at the window like a man with everything to lose. Eventually the glass shattered, and he was able to heave the battered flatscreen through the broken window frame. Seconds later, to an ear-piercingly loud chorus of screams and shrieks, he heard the television smash into oblivion on the sidewalk below.

Grabbing his jacket, smokes, and lighter, he gave his room one last quick once-over and then, with his duffel bag slung over his shoulder, stepped out onto the narrow ledge. Seconds later three police officers, all with their guns drawn, smashed down his door and forced their way into his deserted room— one of them catching a brief glimpse of him as he gingerly inched his way out of the window and out of sight.

"Stop!" the officer yelled, but it was too late.

William was now stuck on a ledge, 5 floors up with a brisk wind snapping at his face. He looked down, sighed heavily, gritted his teeth, and continued to work his way slowly and deliberately, along the narrow ledge, and over towards the nearby ladder to his left, which would, he hoped, give him access to the roof.

Should've stayed retired! he thought to himself, as he looked down to see a rapidly forming congregation of police officers, news anchormen, and pedestrians all looking up at him. He felt nauseous. Sick to the pit of his stomach. What he'd do for a large Americano, a warm slice of apple strudel, and his slippers!

Down below, parked curbside on Deák Ferenc Street within full view of the mayhem unraveling further up the road, Franz, still in his car, enthusiastically watched the situation play out. Starting his engine he slowly pulled away from his parking spot and drove in the direction that William Trevor Francis was now heading.

High up on the ledge, William continued to work his way, inch by inch, closer to the metal rails that would take him to the safety of the rooftop. He was used to heights. They didn't usually faze him. Back in his military days with the 1st RHP, he had jumped tactically a hundred times, probably more. Daytime jumps, nighttime jumps, jumps with full equipment, jumps with full equipment and vehicles—he had enjoyed them all—they had been fun. But now, up here alone, he was feeling decidedly vulnerable with no chute to catch him on the way down if he fell. Standing on a six-inch ledge carrying a hastily packed bag, which was throwing him off balance, he wasn't having any fun at all. *I hate my life. I hate my life,* he repeated to himself. He had been muttering this new mantra ever since he crossed the threshold of broken glass back in his room.

With one last step, he was finally safe with the cold metal of the railing firmly in his grasp. Heaving his bag of equipment over his shoulders, he quickly clambered onto the rooftop and surveyed his surroundings, looking for an escape route. It was too late. Without even having the time to gather his bearings or catch his breath—let alone figure out how the Hell he was going to get out of dodge—the large rooftop access doors flung wide open.

Two officers, Officer Serge and Officer Dmitri, charged through it, their CZ P-09's drawn. He hastily scanned the adjacent rooftops and considered his options. He had one chance, and he took it! Securing the bag onto his back and sprinting with all of his might towards the edge of the building he planted his foot solidly onto the foot-high rooftop ledge and leapt high into the air like an Olympic gold medalist.

Crashing hard onto the neighboring section of rooftop he grabbed his arm and winced at the sharp pain in his chest and legs. Turning around, and to his total dismay, he saw one of the over-zealous younger officers preparing to make the same jump. *There's always one isn't there!* he thought to himself. Catching his breath and resigning himself to the long, protracted chase that he knew would now ensue, he picked himself up and started running along the galvanized steel-clad ridge of the roof's spine.

William Trevor Francis, with a second officer in hot pursuit, continued to run along the roof's metal ridge, purposefully sliding down onto one of the side buildings, dropping 10 feet in the process. Rolling out onto the flat opening, he picked himself up and brushed himself off. *Not bad for an old man* he thought to himself, before continuing to parkour his way through the lightly graveled surface, expertly weaving his way between, over, under, and around the many obstacles in his path.

If it wasn't for the fact that I'm being chased by a cop with a gun this could be fun he thought.

Reaching the building's ledge, he slammed on the brakes and came to a screeching halt. The gap between the two buildings was too great, even for him. He was no James Bond. Close, but no cigar. Looking down, he knew he was trapped, and with the pursuing officers catching up fast, he knew he didn't have many options left. Running his fingers through his hair and with sweat pouring down his face he tried his best to be objective. Taking a long, deep breath that filled his burning, aching lungs to maximum capacity he double-checked for any other alternatives and then, disappointedly, took five steps back.

Advancing at full steam, and with determination painted across his face like Braveheart, he ran forward and planted his foot firmly two inches from the ledge's lip, launching himself high into the air with the early morning sun framing his magnificent silhouette.

Flying like a penguin, his arms and legs flailing in mid-air, he crashed unceremoniously through the fourth storey apartment window he was aiming for. Bursting through the glass window, taking out the curtain and curtain rod in the process, he rolled into the apartment and over the floor. Aching with pain, and laughing in shock and total disbelief at his miraculous good fortune, he picked himself up and slowly got to his feet, brushing the broken glass from his body in the process. The pursuing police officer, thinking twice before attempting the same suicidal stunt decided, instead, to play it safe and called for backup as his red-faced and rotund colleague arrived, gasping frantically for breath, at his side.

With sweat pouring off his face, and with added cuts to his arms and torso, he checked his body for any new serious injuries and then started to repack the items that were falling out of his bag. A large, heavy hairdryer hit him in the back of his head.

"Owww! What the Hell?" he exclaimed in pain, pivoting around to see who had just thrown it.

In front of him, an attractive half-naked woman with rollers in her long, auburn hair had been applying heavy black Amy Winehouse-esque eyeliner at her makeup table. She let out a blood-curdling scream at the top of her lungs. Families all over Eastern Europe must have heard it. William was panicked, frozen to the spot, unable to move. Normally, attractive, semi-nude women were right up his alley. But this was different. This was her turf and he was an intruder, clearly uninvited, and unwanted.

"I'm sorry!" he said, apologetically. He meant it.

Still rubbing his head, he headed towards the main door and opened it, only to close it a split-second later when he heard, once again, the heavy thumping of boots running up the stairs and down the hallway towards him.

He turned to face the woman again, obvious regret and remorse in his eyes. The woman, now reaching for another heavy object to throw, let out a second deafening scream.

"I'm sorry!"

Her hysteria, understandably, continued.

"Tűzlépcső? Fire escape?" He tried desperately to express that he wanted out too.

Seeming to understand that he didn't pose any immediate threat, she pointed to a window on the opposite side of her room. He hurried over to it and looked out, and then looked back at her, appreciatively.

"Thank you!" he said, giving her a grateful smile before throwing his bag onto his back and climbing out of her window, onto the steel grate outside.

He scurried down the stairs like a rat down a drainpipe. Coming to a ladder and utilizing a fireman's descent, he gripped the ladder's side with his feet and slid down to the ground level. He was now in a dark alley with the sound of sirens blaring in the distance.

As he staggered through the dark alleyway, he began thinking about his bigger exit strategy. He was burned. No matter what, he knew he needed to get out of Budapest—and Hungary—as quickly as possible. But first things first. He needed to get out of this alley, and then he needed to get out of this neighborhood. Making his way to the other end of the narrow corridor, banging into the walls, trash cans, and garbage-filled bags in the process he stopped to catch his breath. He was exhausted.

Behind him, advancing slowly up the alley, the black Jaguar with Franz behind the wheel suddenly accelerated, careening towards him, pedal to the metal, honed in on his target. The car quickly picked up pace, fast approaching its intended victim. William turned around when he heard the engine roar and panicked. *What the Hell is happening?* he thought to himself. *I'm in a bloody Hitchcock movie!*

Up ahead, a wire fence blocked his exit. He took a deep breath, secured his bag, and scaled the chain-link fence, swinging his legs up high and dropping to the other side à la Army grapple. Impeded, the Jaguar screeched to a halt, unable to go any further, and started to reverse down the alley from where it had come. Confused but relieved, William rounded the corner out onto what he hoped would be a quiet side street.

Nope! Wrong again! he thought as he walked right into two stationary police cars that were waiting for him. His stomach dropped. *Unbelievable*, he thought. Shaking his head in utter disbelief, he turned, cut, and ran down the street in the opposite direction, the two Mercedes-Benz squad cars, their engines now revved up and ready, peeling into action.

William Trevor Francis, now fully in his stride, with adrenaline and testosterone coursing through his veins in preposterous proportions, ducked behind a parked Skoda, zig-zagged around a pretty decent-looking Audi A6, and changed his direction, once again, for good measure as he sprinted down another quieter side street.

The squad cars slammed on their brakes, clouds of heavy white smoke filling the wheel wells from the burnt rubber of their tires. Up ahead, he could make out the rumbling of 90's Euro rap, and against his better judgment, made a B-Line towards it.

Turning left onto József Attila Utca, he found himself surrounded by three heavily tattooed, rough-looking individuals all hanging around and admiring a pimped-out, crappy-looking, 1990's era convertible 3 Series BMW. He didn't know whether to be more intimidated by them, or by the monstrosity they had Frankensteined. A fourth guy, presumably the creator of this abomination, was behind the wheel giving the car plenty of gas. With the engine rumbling and grinding, and with incredibly bad Euro rap music blowing out everyone's eardrums, none of them saw or heard him coming.

Using all of his skill and remaining energy, he cross-body

tackled the first man, knocking him into the other two like bowling pins. They crashed to the ground, cursing and confused, completely unaware of what had just hit them. Without missing a beat, he tossed his bag into the back of the open car, jumped in, and drop-kicked the unexpecting driver clean out of the driver's side door with a throwaway "Sorry mate!"

Slamming the door shut with a finishing stroke, he engaged first gear, rammed his foot onto the accelerator, and 'drove it like he stole it'.

The tires screeched, and spun, as the car jettisoned away down the busy street, the heavy white smoke of burning rubber once again filling the air.

CHAPTER SEVEN

DON'T HASSEL THE HOFF

As WILLIAM TREVOR FRANCIS ACCELERATED DOWN Andrássy Avenue, the report of the suspect in a stolen BMW 325i convertible was already being broadcast over the police scanners. Within a matter of minutes, he had been spotted. The chase through the neighborhood streets of Terézváros, up past Hero's Square, over and around the Oktogon intersection, and down Király Street was on! One by one, blue and white police cars joined the caravan of sirens and flashing lights, in hot pursuit of their suspect.

Weaving his way through a stream of motorists, he crossed up onto the sidewalk, and with a heavy hand on the horn, flew through each and every obstacle in his path doing his best to avoid the pedestrians, and vendors, who were all screaming, diving for cover and jumping out of his way. Skillfully maneuvering his BMW back onto the street he rocketed through an intersection of red lights, causing a small number of other cars to swerve, skid, and crash in their attempts to avoid hitting him.

Expertly working the clutch, he popped the gears up into fourth, down into second, and then, turning a sharp right-hand corner onto Vörösmarty Street, engaged third, the car drifting hard and then straightening out as he rocketed past the historic WWII House of Terror Museum on his right.

Up ahead, still riding the horn and accelerator simultaneously, he spotted a parking structure, and without hesitation, slammed on the brakes, shoved his gears down into second, yanked back on his handbrake, and skidded into the parking structure, smashing through the wooden entrance barrier in the process.

Once inside, he didn't let up. He couldn't afford to. Time was now his enemy. Darting and weaving his way around the rows of parked cars and shopping-laden pedestrians, he speedily climbed his way up the parking structure levels, a squad of sirens only seconds behind him.

Hitting the 5th floor, he turned the incredibly tight corner and headed over to a dimly lit section of the structure on the far side. Slamming on the brakes, he fish-tailed the car into an empty parking spot, a maneuver that would have made The Transporter green with envy. *Not bad* he thought to himself, genuinely impressed by the car's capabilities. *That doesn't suck!*

Without wasting any time he grabbed his bag from the back seat, exited the vehicle, ran over to the stairwell, and then hastily made his way down the two flights of stairs to the 3rd floor just before the pursuing fleet of cars had time to catch up with him. Walking out onto the deserted floor he breathed deeply, composed himself, and then casually strolled through the sea of parked cars testing the door handles of each one as he passed. On the fifth attempt, he managed to open the door to a 1980's Skoda Estelle and jumped behind the wheel.

The last police car to enter the parking structure flew up the ramp with its sirens blazing, skidded around the corner, and immediately slammed on its brakes grinding to an abrupt, tire-screeching halt. The police driver, furious at the moron behind the wheel of the dirty brown Skoda—which was slowly backing out of a parking bay and blocking his path—honked heavily on his horn.

"Get out of the way!" he shouted.

William quickly did as he was told, stopped reversing, and immediately pulled forward allowing the police car to roar past. Once out of sight, he put the car back into reverse and slowly eased his way out of the parking bay again, leisurely chugging his way towards the down ramp and the structure's exit.

As he descended the exit ramp, a train of even more police cars raced past him in the opposite direction. Holding his breath, and sitting as low as he possibly could in his seat, he slowly sputtered down to the ground level, through the broken barrier, and out onto the street.

Franz, his eyes as vigilant as ever in his black Jaguar, continued to cruise up and down outside the parking lot, searching every side alley and parked vehicle for his prey, oblivious to the fact that William Trevor Francis had just driven right past him.

———————

Back at the Ritz-Carlton, a young police officer, notepad in hand, was questioning the receptionist, Amie Zezulka, at the hotel front desk, as well as the bellboy and any other hotel employees who had come into contact with the suspect. The officer took detailed notes while other police officers around him questioned the hotel manager and hotel guests in turn.

"And what can you tell me about the appearance of the subject, a Mr. Nicholas Allen?" he asked her. "How did he pay? How long did he plan on staying?"

Amie didn't like this guy or his tone. She found him rude and unnecessarily curt.

"He was a regular customer. Been here for a week. Tall, well dressed. *Polite*." She stopped, thought for a split second, and then continued, a slight smile on her face.

"And very confident," she added.

"Was there anything unusual about him? His demeanor? Anything that stood out? Any distinguishing features? Anything he said that seemed out of place or strange?"

"No," she responded. "He was English. Handsome. A gentleman."

A fellow officer interrupted him, whispering into his ear.

"Thank you for your time Ms. Zezulka. I'll let you know if we need anything else."

With that, he closed his book, stowed his pen, and walked over to the team of forensics who had just finished wiping down Suite 529 for prints and any other relevant information they could glean from its previous occupant.

It had been a long day. With the sun now setting, William Trevor Francis continued his drive through the Czech Republic, headed North on E461, towards the German border on his long drive back to Berlin. With a cigarette hanging from his parched and cracked lips he looked beaten and tired. He turned the radio dial, trying to stay awake but even the saccharin-sweet bubble-gum pop music that he was listening to couldn't do the trick. He nodded off, the long piercing honk from an oncoming truck waking him abruptly from his slumber. With an instinctive swerve, he managed to veer the car back into its lane, just in the nick of time. A close call. Too close for comfort.

Rolling down the window for some fresh air and blinking his eyes repeatedly to wake himself up, he checked the car's fuel gauge. He was close to empty. Pulling off the main road at the first gas station he could find, he filled his car and strolled into the Agip convenience mart. Looking around he quickly scanned the inside for trouble. There was none. The small gas station convenience store, on the outskirts of Brno, was empty, save for the early twenty-year-old kid who was working the cash register.

Slowly walking the aisles, he grabbed a cheap T-shirt with a dated but beautifully coiffed image of David Hasselhoff on its front, a pack of band-aids, ibuprofen pills, some gauze swabs, and a bottle of medical alcohol from the shelf before entering the restroom.

Verifying that he was alone, he locked the door and took a long look at himself in the mirror. He looked like shit. *What a mess* he thought to himself, his head hung low in dismay, shaking from side to side in disapproval. Placing the contents of his arms on the counter next to the washbasin, he turned on the taps, washed his face, and removed his blood-stained sweater revealing the many open cuts and black and blue bruises that he had amassed since the explosion. Cleaning and dressing his wounds to the best of his abilities for the second time that day, he took a small handful of pills, knocked them back with a swig of water, put on his clean T-shirt, and ran his fingers through his hair in an effort to make himself look as presentable as possible. Easier said than done. Tossing the blood-stained sweater and swabs into the nearby trash, he took one last long look at himself in the mirror. He still looked like shit.

He shook his head at the campy, wannabe rock star image reflected back at him on his chest. *Just when I thought it couldn't get any worse I've got the bloody Hoff's face staring back at me!* he thought to himself.

Deep down he actually had quite a bit of respect for Germany's poster boy, having been a huge fan of the Knight Rider television series growing up in the early '80s, but wearing a T-shirt of him was just taking it too far. Way too far. And he wasn't even in Germany!

Exiting the bathroom with his belongings in hand, he walked over to the cold drinks section. After a quick stop at the snacks aisle, he ambled over to the counter juggling the bottle of soda, chips, and all the other supplies he had taken and used without paying for. Dumping his items unceremoniously onto the counter, he motioned with his finger towards the bank of cigarettes behind the kid who he now noticed had short ginger hair. *Poor bastard,* he thought to himself. *No one likes a ginger.*

"Camel. Blue," he said. More of an instruction than a request.

The spotty youth tossed the pack of smokes onto the counter and started to slowly punch the prices into the cash register. As he did so, William noticed the sleek black security camera which was hanging from the ceiling next to a small TV monitor. He stared blankly at the screen, mindlessly watching a Gambrinus beer commercial playing on it.

"You paying in korunas or Euros?" the cashier asked.

"Euros."

"Eighty-three ninety-eight," the cashier said, his mind not quite made up about the dubious-looking character in front of him.

"Bloody Hell," he exclaimed. "That's daylight robbery!"

The kid looked back at him with the most uninterested

expression he could muster. There was no need for words. The kid's '*not my problem*' expression had said it all.

William reached for his wallet and placed two 50 Euro bills on the counter. He glanced back up at the TV monitor. The commercials had stopped. Now it was back to the news. A young female reporter, bundled up in a stylishly tailored plum-colored trench coat and gripping a handheld mic, was speaking in front of the Budapest Police Department Headquarters.

"… local police officials are turning up the heat on the manhunt for a suspected terrorist linked to the bombing at the Allied Laboratories here in the heart of the city …"

A blurry photo popped up on the screen. The cashier, who had carefully been studying the battered and bruised man in front of him, turned his attention towards the TV, and then back to his customer. William watched him cautiously.

"My change?" William asked, trying to divert the kid's attention away from the news broadcast.

"Eh? Oh sure."

The cashier started to count out the change but stopped halfway through.

"You got some nasty cuts there," he said.

"Work's killing me," William responded, giving the best fake smile he could manage.

A composite drawing came up on the TV screen, this time grabbing both of their attention. The artist's rendition of a dark-haired man looked a lot like William Trevor Francis. The news reporter continued.

"The suspect is believed to be a British male in his mid to late forties, about six foot tall, and approximately two hundred pounds. This man is extremely dangerous. We encourage anyone who sees him not to approach him but to contact the police immediately."

William knew it was time to split.

"Keep the change," he told the cashier, before grabbing his goods and exiting the store.

As soon as he left, the young kid looked up again at the TV, double-checked to see that his customer in the Skoda Estelle had pulled out of the forecourt, and satisfied that he was gone, picked up the phone to the local police station.

———————

FIFTEEN MINUTES LATER, POLICE OFFICERS WERE AT THE Agip gas station questioning the cashier in precise detail. Having confirmed the time frame, the direction in which the driver was heading, the purchases he had made as well as his general attitude and demeanor, the questioning officer asked the cashier for the store's security tape.

"I'm going to need your video footage," he told the kid.

"Sure," the kid stammered. "It's in the back. I'll get it for you."

"No worries. One of our men can get it." The police officer cut him off and gestured to his colleague.

"Is there anything else you remember? Anything unusual about his looks or his behavior?"

The young kid hesitated, thinking long and hard for any new details he could provide.

"Well, he used the bathroom to clean himself up. He looked like shit."

CHAPTER EIGHT

GIVE IT UP FOR CINDY

BACK IN BERLIN AND AFTER AN INCREDIBLY LONG AND tiring 11-hour drive—after Brno, he had decided to avoid all major roads and had even been forced to pull over on the outskirts of Dresden to rest—William Trevor Francis was now parked outside the seedy-looking Club Exotica on the corner of Kantstrasse and Windscheidstrasse to the West of the city.

Finishing his smoke, he ground the butt into the center console ashtray and drank the remnants of his now warm and flat Diet Coke. It was 6:30 pm and time for some answers.

Grabbing his jacket, which given the recent turn of events was looking a little worse for wear, he slammed the car door shut behind him. Walking up to the large Tardis blue-colored doors, crowned with the matching blue fluorescent light of the club's name, he wondered to himself how the night was going to play out.

An impressive, 6'6" black muscle-bound monster of a man greeted him at the door. *If Dwayne Johnson was 'The Rock' then this guy was 'The Bloody Mountain'* he thought to himself, undeterred and mildly impressed by the guy's daunting physique and athleticism.

"Hello tiny," he said flippantly, hoping that Godzilla couldn't speak English.

Paying his 10 Euros to the female bondage-clad ticket attendant with more piercings than sense, he pulled back the heavy dark blue velvet curtain and opened the tatty-looking door it was hiding.

The inside was your usual low to mid-range strip club. Two stages each with two baby oil greased poles at either end of them, and a row of small dimly lit tables, intimate booths, private benches, and several private rooms, all flanked on the left-hand side by a well-stocked and insanely overpriced bar. He felt right at home!

Still wearing his Hasselhoff T-shirt, he made his way to the front of the left-hand stage, closest to the bar, and grabbed a seat. The club was half empty but would surely pick up later that night. That's if the goddamn techno music crap that was blaring through the speakers didn't drive the customers away first.

He signaled to a waitress and took out his smokes.

"Rauchen verboten," the waitress told him as soon as she saw him about to spark up.

"No worries," he responded, "Not a big deal," and put his smokes and lighter back in his pocket.

After ordering his customary 'Johnnie Walker Black. Double. Rocks on the side' he sat back in his chair, admired the semi-nude women gyrating in front of him, and checked his watch again. It was now 6:48 pm. *That bastard should be here soon* he thought to himself.

The D.J. working from a narrow black felt-covered booth to the right of the bar lowered the volume to announce the next dancer.

"Auf der Hauptbühne, Applaus für Cindyyyyy!"

William, battered, unshaven, tired, and with heavy bags under his eyes looked terrible and felt even worse, but all of that was about to change. He was soon going to feel like a million bucks! The music started again, but this time, the techno garbage playing before had mercifully been replaced by Destiny's Child 'Bootylicious'. *Yeah, I can handle this,* he chuckled to himself, a reference to the song's opening lyrics.

Appearing from behind the velvet curtain, a bikini-clad dancer in her mid-30's stepped up onto the stage, grabbed the nearest pole, and spun, sex-on-legs, to a round of rapturous applause and wolf whistles. *Absolutely stunning!* he thought to himself. *Jessica Rabbit in the flesh.*

Whipping and tossing her long vibrantly colored red hair, she worked the stage like the pro that she was, kicking, bending, squatting, and sliding under the torrent of Euro bills that was raining down upon her. He was mesmerized. Totally captivated. There *was* a God after all.

Removing her bejeweled top and easing into her sensual stride, she smiled at him and worked her way over to his area. His drink arrived and was placed on the table, but he didn't even notice. He didn't even care.

"How you been keeping?" he asked her when she finally stopped in front of him. Her tanned body and toned torso glistened with the slightest hint of perspiration. She looked amazing and smelt divine—her candy-sweet perfume, synonymous with strippers, hanging heavily in the air.

"Better than you. You look terrible," she winked.

William grinned and, noticing his drink for the first time, plonked two ice cubes into it. He took a long slow sip, savoring every single second.

"I haven't seen you in a while. Where have you been?" she asked.

"Busy. You want to catch up sometime?"

She smiled.

"Yes, I'd like that."

"Great, I've just got to sort out a bit of business with your boss first."

"OK. You know where I am," she smiled.

Cindy and William 'had history'. A number of years back, when she had first started dancing at the Club Exotica, William had immediately 'fallen in love' with her. Not that he had actually *fallen in love* with her in the real sense—not even the dumbest asshole does that—but, being single and alone, he had allowed himself to become close with this street-smart, sexy, and sassy young woman.

Learning that she, and her 2-year-old son Max, were both in an abusive relationship with her perpetually drunk and violent partner, he had forcefully inserted himself into her affairs, kicked the living shit out of the bastard, and helped her and her kid relocate to a quieter, safer and more suitable neighborhood.

The kid wasn't his of course, and he felt no financial obligation towards her, but being able to help them both, no strings attached and no re-payment necessary made him feel good about himself. It was a simple act of kindness that he could afford, and which had dramatically changed the lives of two innocent and deserving individuals.

He removed a stack of bills from his pocket and slipped her a couple of hundred and a warm smile.

"Treat yourself and get a little something for Max."

Thanking him, she blew him a kiss and continued to work the stage, scooping up her tips from the dance floor and working the other men and women in 'the kill zone'. *What a woman!* he thought to himself as he took another sip from his glass. *What an absolute knockout!*

———————————

Fifteen minutes later, William noticed Vinny entering his club—the purpose for his early evening visit. Finishing his drink and leaving a 20 under the empty glass, he got up and walked over to the bar where Vinny was chatting up the bartender.

"We need to talk. Now!" he said, grabbing Vinny roughly by the arm, and manhandling him into his office in the rear of the club, out of view of the club's patrons.

"Get your hands off me! What the Hell do you think you're doing?" Vinny exclaimed, caught off-guard and unaware.

Once in the quiet privacy of the office, William abruptly pushed Vinny into his oversized office chair and leaned, menacingly, over him.

"Who put you up to it?" he asked. Anger, and a sense of betrayal, slowly bubbling to a boil within him—a lethal combination for most men—doubly so for him.

"What the Hell are you talking about? Calm down, Will. I swear I don't know what you mean."

William knew all too well from personal experience that Vinny had the gift of the gab and could easily talk himself into—and out of—any situation he wanted to. He wasn't going to fall for it. Unconvinced with the response, he grabbed Vinny's right hand, secured it firmly in his grasp, and broke a finger, snapping it like a cheap plastic straw. Vinny yelled out in pain and shock.

"Jesus Christ! You asshole!" he shouted.

"Vinny, I'm not going to ask you again. You know that!"

"Alright, alright, just calm the Hell down. Jesus!"

Vinny squirmed in his seat. Looking forlornly at his broken, and rapidly swelling index finger he started to confess.

"It was a job from a guy called Victor. But I don't know any more than that, I swear Will."

Still unsatisfied, William applied a little more pressure to the busted appendage. Vinny winced and continued through spit and gritted teeth.

"Ok. Ok. All I know is he's one of us, ex-Para, maybe Legion."

"Go on." William was listening intently.

"Word is he did a couple of tours in Africa. Made himself a lot of money running guns to both sides. I sold him some gear from our supplies back in the early days before he went solo and upped his game. It was easy money."

"Where do I come into this?" he asked. Vinny continued reluctantly.

"It was a simple job. Said he needed the best. I didn't think anything of it—break into a lab, steal some stupid files, destroy the joint—easy, especially for someone like you. I swear it's the truth, Will."

William wasn't buying it.

"Why me?"

Vinny—with the pain in his finger slowly subsiding, and his head getting clearer—was beginning to feel a little more confident in his composure.

"Like I said, he wanted the best. Like it or not mate, you've got a bit of a reputation these days. All the wrong people know you're out there. How do you think I'm able to get you the jobs in the first place?"

William thought for a moment, processing the information.

"Get in touch with him and set up a meeting."

"I can't do that, Will. I don't have access to the guy like that. I told you, he came to me."

William applied a little 'gentle persuasion' to another of Vinny's fingers.

"Wrong answer. Try again."

"Son of a bitch! Alright, alright!"

William released the pressure and relaxed his grip around Vinny's middle finger.

"He's putting on a fight in two days' time. There's big money involved. You'll find him there for sure."

He reached into his inside pocket but William stopped him, mid-process, with a brutal backhand slap.

"It's my goddamn business card! The details are on it!" Vinny explained, frustrated but also very aware of how William could react.

Retrieving the blue and neon pink Club Exotica business card for himself, William flipped it over, and read the chicken-scratch writing on the back detailing the address and date of the upcoming underground fight.

"The next time you set me up with a bullshit job I'm going to get violent with you," he said matter-of-factly.

Vinny raised his broken finger.

"What the Hell do you call this?" he shouted as William got up, turned, and headed out the door.

"A warning."

OUTSIDE THE CLUB, SITTING IN HIS BLACK JAGUAR WHICH had been neatly tucked around the corner and out of sight, Franz turned down the volume to Rachmaninoff's Piano Concerto No.2: Adagio Sostenuto, which he had been quietly listening to, picked up his cell phone and made a call.

"You were right. He's just left the club," he confirmed.

Acknowledging the response on the other end of the line, he dutifully hung up, removed his 9mm pistol and suppressor from the glove box, exited the car, and crossed the non-descript side street towards the strip club's entrance.

Back in his office, Vinny was nursing his broken finger over a large glass of cheap Polish vodka.

"Who the Hell are you?" he shouted in anger at the man who had just walked in unannounced and uninvited.

Franz said nothing, but simply raised his gun and fired two short rounds into Vinny's pink perplexed face.

CHAPTER NINE

THE PLOT THICKENS

LOCATED IN THE MITTE DISTRICT OF BERLIN, ONLY A ten-minute walk from Checkpoint Charlie, William Trevor Francis, hiding in plain sight, sat at his cheap IKEA-esque table-top and poured himself a stiff drink. He drained it in one gulp, poured himself a second, lit a cigarette, and inhaled deeply—the bright neon sign of the two-star hotel he was staying at casting a boudoir red glow across his tired and haggard face. He booted up his laptop and sighed heavily. He needed more information. He somehow needed to figure out the bigger picture. *How had the police been able to track him down so quickly? How did they even know who he was?* These were the two main questions he was dying to get to the bottom of.

Hitting the keyboard keys hard and fast, he ran his sur-veillance software program once more and accessed the INTERPOL mainframe server for the second time that week. *This program's genius,* he thought to himself, unsure exactly of how it worked—just grateful that it did—and continued working his way through the directories.

As soon as he had access to the DRI folders, he located and selected the Allied Laboratories one and opened it, various images and photos immediately populating his screen. He clicked and dragged them, one by one, to the left of his monitor so that he could study them collectively alongside their corresponding notes and comments. Selecting, and enlarging, an image of a charred body with a file number and the name MARIE BOYER under it, he shook his head in regret, not for anything that *he* had done specifically, but for the loss of what he suspected was an innocent life.

Scotch in hand, he continued to click on the individual thumbnails, slowly putting together the jigsaw puzzle, a patchwork of facts and delicate details that he hoped would soon yield answers. Clicking on a folder named 'Suspects' he stopped, the blood immediately draining from his face, when he saw that it only contained one file with the name 'Suspect: Francis, William Trevor' on it. *WTF?* he thought to himself.

Opening it with bated breath he stared, apprehensively, not only at the same roadside photos that Monique Lefort had shared with her team of DRI agents just a few days earlier in Paris, but also at the newly added gas station still shots and DNA evidence linking him directly to his most recent activities.

'Blood found at the site of the explosion also matches blood samples found at The Ritz Carlton, the abandoned BMW, and the AGIP Gas Station'.

"What the Hell is going on?!" he exclaimed aloud, to an empty audience.

'Multiple larceny counts'; 'grand theft auto'; 'numerous high-end robberies'; 'International thief wanted throughout Europe'; 'suspect also on Scotland Yard list - priority HIGH'; 'considered armed and extremely dangerous'.

William leapt up from his chair in a fit of panic and bewilderment, his mind now awash with a booze-fueled concoction of confusion and paranoia.

Gripping the side of the table to stabilize his stance he retraced every minute detail in his head. Every spoken word from Vinny. Every process of his detailed, methodical, OCD-like planning and preparation. *What was the link?* he asked himself, repeating the same question again and again in his head as he paced up and down the close confines of his cramped hotel room. Slowly, fragment by fragment, shard by shard, the stark truth of what had happened began to dawn on him. He had been framed. From the beginning. It must have all been an elaborate ploy to play him. Only, he presumed, he was supposed to have died in the explosion. *Yes,* he thought, *of course!* That would have tied everything up neatly. But he hadn't!

Back at his desk, rocking in his chair with a belly full of adrenaline and growing anger, he pulled up a database search on the name 'VICTOR'.

———

LATER THAT SAME EVENING IN BERLIN, POLICE AUTHORITIES and forensics teams had shut down and taken over the Club Exotica, a multitude of police cars along with inquisitive and intrusive pedestrians congregating outside. Vinny's stiff and lifeless body was being zipped up in a large, black body bag and heaved onto a gurney. The club was a confusing blend of ambulance men, bikini-clad strippers, malcontent patrons, and semi-nude employees—all being questioned against their will by Berlin's finest men in blue under a canopy of red spotlights.

Front and center was Cindy, now talking to a second officer, giving exactly the same details as she'd given the first, about a particular patron who the waitress and bar staff had witnessed her interacting with earlier that evening.

"And then he saw the deceased enter the club and immediately left you and approached the bar. Is that correct?" the officer asked.

"Yes," Cindy responded calmly. "He saw Vinny and went over to him. And then they both went into his office".

"And you saw this man grab the owner in a confrontational manner? Other witnesses say there was a minor altercation and that he seemed overly aggressive."

"I didn't see that," she continued. "He was in a good mood with me. I'm not saying it *didn't* happen, I'm just saying I didn't *see* it happen."

The officer continued to take notes.

"Do you know the suspect's name?" he asked.

Cindy hesitated. She genuinely believed that her handsome

Englishman was innocent and that they were barking up the wrong tree. In fact, she was certain of it.

"He always asked me to call him Will, that's all I know."

The questioning continued, relentlessly.

"How well do you know the suspect? This 'Will'?"

"Not that well. He sometimes comes in but he hasn't been in for a while. I hardly know him," she responded, now defensively.

"And how would you describe your level of intimacy with him? How much time or attention would you normally give him, compared to your other customers?"

"About the same as normal. He's a nice guy. Generous. Kind. Caring. One of the good ones if you know what I mean."

The officer smirked. *Yeah, sure!* he thought to himself. *One of the good ones, until he pulls out a gun and shoots someone point-blank in the face!*

"How did he know the owner? What was their relationship like? Did there appear to be any malice or ill will between the two of them?" he continued, not letting up.

"No. Like I already said, they knew each other, but I don't know how close. I don't know what more I can tell you," Cindy said, before breaking down into tears, the shock and reality of the situation now hitting home hard.

"Alright. Let me get the sketch artist over and together you can put together an image of what this guy looks like."

With that, the police officer walked away and pencil-man moved in.

IN THE EARLY HOURS OF THE MORNING, BACK AT THE main Berlin police station on the Platz Der Luftbrücke, images and details from the previous night's strip club murder were now being collated, verified, and uploaded onto the station's main server. The processing of all new information was always a tedious and time-consuming endeavor, but someone had to do it. That morning, the responsibility had fallen on the shoulders of a young and dedicated individual called Christoph.

Realizing the similarities between this case's main suspect and the details of an internal memo that had come down from his superior the day before, he accessed the main computer files and, following his hunch, pulled up the internal memo citing the active INTERPOL investigation. He double-checked the artist's composite drawing in his hands. He was right. They matched!

The explosion and murder at the Allied Laboratories in Budapest; the cat and mouse chase over the Ritz-Carlton rooftop; the forced intrusion and damage incurred at a private residence; the carjacking and subsequent car chase through the streets of Budapest and the sighting at an Agip gas station on the outskirts of Brno—some 200 kilometers southeast of Prague—in the Czech Republic were all connected. From the description and details given, it appeared that the same man was indeed wanted for questioning in all instances. Dropping everything, he immediately notified his Senior Officer. Not only had he made a connection, but he also had a name. The five previous cases and now the death of Vinny Menard at his club could all be linked. He had a detailed and singular time-line of events leading right back to Berlin.

HALF AN HOUR LATER, MONIQUE LEFORT, SITTING behind her Paris desk, hung up the telephone. She stared, ob-sessively, at the pinboard hanging from her office wall—heav-ily laden with photos and testimonials, all connecting a series of crimes to her main suspect: William Trevor Francis. This is what she lived for. The hunt. The chase. With the Head of Department in Berlin now sending her all of the information they had from the Club Exotica, everything was slowly starting to come together. Her file on William Trevor Francis was get-ting fatter. This goose was going to get plucked!

CHAPTER TEN

WHO THE HELL ARE YOU?

WILLIAM CHECKED HIS WATCH. IT HAD JUST GONE 8:10 pm, and having tracked down Victor to the secret underground fighting ring on the outskirts of Berlin that Vinny had told him about, he was now waiting patiently in his parked car, hidden from view on a deserted side road, a cigarette in his mouth and Vinny's business card in his hand. On the passenger seat next to him was his open laptop showing a recent mugshot of Victor.

Grabbing his high-definition military binoculars he exited the car and stealthily made his way around to the lip of a small grass-tufted ridge. Taking his position on the damp and cold ground, he carefully observed the activities of the large weather-worn wooden structure a quarter of a mile away—a bustle of activity with various cars arriving and armed guards patrolling. *A tight place to break into* he thought.

Heading back to his car he stowed his affairs, pulled up the collar to his leather jacket, and mindful of attracting any unwanted attention, slowly and carefully made his way along the building's perimeter, past two guards and towards an entrance that he had detected at the rear of the barn. Time to join the party.

Staying in the blackness of the shadows and carefully observing a nearby guard with slicked-back hair, and a week's worth of stubble on his cold sullen face, William waited.

Taking in his surroundings and measuring the distance between himself and the guard, who he now observed was carrying what looked like a small Uzi Pro, he seized his opportunity and charged the man from behind. Taking out his legs with a deft sweep, and catching his neck firmly between his left forearm and upper chest, he slowly applied pressure and squeezed with his right arm until the body fell silently onto the ground beside him, motionless.

Removing a Glock 9mm from the guard's hip—he could easily have taken the Uzi Pro but, gorgeous as it was, it was just too much weapon for what he wanted—he checked that the magazine had all 10 rounds—much easier to count down your ammo when you know how many you're starting with—and wasting no time, entered the building and made his way towards the loud jeering, taunting, and shouting, emanating from within.

Once inside, remaining ever vigilant and as inconspicuous as possible, he worked the crowd and assessed the situation. Two men in the middle of the floor were engaged in a bare-knuckle fight. A crowd of dangerous and highly excited observers were shouting obscenities and encouragement at them both in equal measure. William had done his fair share of fighting in the past, and actually considered himself a pretty damn good opponent, but these two guys were insane. *Nope!* he thought to himself. *If one of those nutters comes at me I'm definitely using my gun.*

Scanning the crowd, and making a mental note of the many armed guards inside the building, he eventually located Victor in the crowd, flanked by two equally ugly, gun-toting associates. A loud cheer erupted from the fighting pit as one of the fighters, a bald, bare-chested, and blood-soaked individual, fell unconscious to the ground, an almighty blow to the face having knocked the living daylights—along with several teeth—out of him. Without wasting a beat, the second fighter was already on top of him, straddling him, and pinning him down, repeatedly and mercilessly pummeling his face, blow after blow. *He obviously hadn't got the memo that he's already won* William thought to himself with a 'rather him than me' shrug of his shoulders.

All of a sudden, presumably having found his unconscious colleague outside, a lone guard forced his way through the crowds and into the middle of the melee, shouting at the top of his lungs.

"Vorsicht! We've got company!"

Within seconds the fight and the room had broken apart, and everyone had split the scene, each hastily making their way out of the building and off the premises in an 'every man for himself' retreat.

William Trevor Francis, tailing Victor from a distance, followed him out of the building, out to the parking lot, and out into a frenzy of peeling tires, smoke, and dust. As Victor and his two lackeys got into their car, he quickly set off on foot to his own vehicle to follow them.

───────────

PULLING UP OUTSIDE A SMALL, DARK AND EMPTY CAFÉ bar in the Lichterfelde neighborhood just off Lausanner Strasse, William turned off his ignition, killed his lights, and observed as the three men entered the building, gestured to the barman, and made their way down towards the back of the room.

His stomach was rumbling. He was starving. *When was the last time he ate something?* he asked himself, unsure of when or what he had last shoved into his mouth. A hot dog was what he wanted right now. Yes. With all the trimmings. A beer-cooked bratwurst, with a mountain of sauerkraut, and lashings of thick yellow mustard. And two steins of pilsner to wash it all down. *Yes!* he thought. That's what he needed right about now! His stomach growled in hungry anticipation. It would have to wait.

Exiting his car, with the Glock secured in his waistband, he approached the café and walked in, the small polished brass bell hanging above the door signaling his arrival as he opened it. He approached the bar, taking a mental note of the two elderly gentlemen playing backgammon in the front left-hand corner of the room, and ordered a drink.

WHO THE HELL ARE YOU?

"Scotch. Johnnie Black. Double."

The barman, a medium-sized, shifty, and slightly over-weight individual in his early 50's grabbed the bottle, and non-communicatively poured and placed the drink in front of him.

"Danke." William said, followed by "Toiletten?"

The barman eyed him cautiously and then nodded towards the back of the room.

William crossed the room, turned down the corridor, and saw the men's toilets on the left. He carefully opened the door and saw that they were empty. There were two other doors remaining. Removing his gun, checking the chamber, and flicking the safety switch to off, he slowly pried open the second door on his right. A supply room. He continued, his senses now on full alert, towards the third and final door at the bottom of the dark hallway. He paused, the hairs on his forearms bristling, as he listened to the sound of voices coming from within. Taking a breath, and calming his nerves, he composed himself, took a beat, and opened the door.

In two quick successive shots, fired with cold military precision, he shot the two men as they were reaching for their weapons. Victor, sitting in his dark leather padded chair alone, and unprotected, made a sudden move for his own gun but William, cool, calm, and collected, already had him in his sights.

"Put it down," he said.

"Who the Hell are you? Do you know who I am?"

William wasn't in the mood for egos.

"I said put it down. Now!" the stern authority of someone who is fully in control of their situation evident in his voice.

Slowly, Victor did what he was told and begrudgingly placed his gun on the table in front of him. Wasting no time, William grabbed it and stuffed it into his jacket pocket. Hearing the heavy thud of footsteps in the hallway, and realizing that someone else was quickly approaching the room, he deftly stepped back behind the door and out of sight, milliseconds before the barman barged into the room with his shotgun at the ready. Catching him unaware, William forcibly body-slammed him up against the wall, and efficiently cold-cocked him with the butt of his pistol. The barman instantly dropped to the ground, unconscious. William, undeterred, and unphased, turned back to Victor.

"Who set me up?"

"I don't know what you're talking about. Go to Hell!"

William trained his gun on Victor's right shoulder, and fired a singular shot, the black bullet hole slowly seeping red sticky blood down Victor's chest.

Victor let out a blood-curdling scream, a mixture of shock, and disbelief.

"You're mad! I'll kill you for this!"

William trained his gun on Victor's left shoulder and fired again. Victor yelled in excruciating pain. Calmly walking over to him, William sat on the table's edge and looked Victor defiantly in the eyes. He rested the muzzle of his still smoking gun on Victor's right knee in a Dirty Harry 'Make my day' kind of way.

"I won't ask again. I know you approached Vinny with the Allied Lab job, and I know that it was a stitch-up. Now what I want to know is who put you up to it, and why."

Victor wasn't going to spill the beans that easily.

"You're mad. You're a dead man. You don't stand a chance."

Pushing the gun muzzle firmly into Victor's kneecap, William leaned over, and with his left hand, squeezed Victor's shoulder, digging his thumb deep into the bullet wound as far as it would go.

"Talk!"

Victor screamed out in agonizing pain but refused to buckle.

Mildly impressed with the guy's resolve, but in no mood to play games, he pulled the trigger.

"I said talk!"

Victor, let out a horrific, gut-wrenching scream. With a cold film of sweat covering his body, Victor, now going into shock from the loss of blood, reluctantly gave up a name.

"Franz. Franz Hagen. His name's Franz Hagen."

"Who is he? Who does he work for?" William sensed that time was running out. The guy would soon pass out.

Victor had no more fight left in him. His resolve had left the building along with his kneecap.

"All I know is he works for a guy called Sinclair."

Victor's head was beginning to sag, the guy was drifting. William gave him a quick sharp slap across the face to wake him up.

"Where can I find him?"

"I don't know. He'll find you," Victor said, spitting at William in utter contempt.

Wiping his face, William searched Victor's pockets and removed his cell phone. He flipped it open and scrolled through the recent call log.

"Not if I find him first."

Satisfied, he got up, pocketed the cell phone, and turned to leave. As he opened the door and walked back out into the empty, dark corridor, Victor taunted him one last time.

"I'll kill you for this. I swear I'll make you suffer. I'll kill you, and everyone you've ever cared about."

Outside the room, William hesitated, considered Victor's threat, and stepped back in. Firing a single shot, he exited the room for a second time and closed the door behind him.

No, you won't, he thought to himself. *Not anymore!*

Walking back down the dark corridor, he approached the bar where his scotch was still waiting for him, drained it in one thirsty gulp, and turned to face the two patrons. The elderly gentlemen looked back expressionlessly at him. Approaching them with his head held high, and his shoulders back, he defiantly stared them both down. They quickly understood the gravity of their predicament. They had seen nothing. With their heads now hung low, William confidently walked past them, and out onto the dark night streets.

CHAPTER ELEVEN
ALLONS-Y!

LATER THAT SAME EVENING, WITH REPORTS OF GUNFIRE having been called into the local station, police, forensics, a photographer, and a coroner were all at the scene of the café bar diligently carrying out their respective roles. Three dead bodies were all being photographed and tagged—two on the floor, and the third, Victor, slumped in his chair. The bartender, now cuffed, and with a seriously large bandage over his head, was being taken away for further questioning down at the station.

The lead officer at the scene was desperately trying to piece everything together. The deceased was a notorious villain, involved in numerous unsavory activities including illegal gambling, prostitution, drug trafficking, and racketeering. *Plenty of people would be happy to see him dead,* he thought, *but who would have the balls to kill him?* With no witnesses available to shed light on that evening's occurrences, he was genuinely perplexed. *The second shooting in as many days? Could they be related?*

———————

THREE DAYS LATER, HAVING SUCCESSFULLY DEPARTED
Berlin and arrived in Paris, William Trevor Francis was sitting
in a small one-bedroom apartment overlooking the Crémaillère
restaurant on the Place du Tertre in the 18th arrondissement,
the magnificent white-lined Sacré-Coeur basilica looming
majestically in the background. He loved Montmartre, the
quaint narrow cobble-lined streets, the bustle of vendors, art-
ists, and tourists. The cafés, bakeries, and restaurants—and
at the bottom of the hill in stark contrast to the cathedral at
its summit—the dark, dangerous, and seedy streets of Pigalle,
heaving with hookers, sex shops, and sin.

William had been raised and educated in the South of
England, but he had been born in the 92nd arrondissement of
Asnières-Sur-Seine to the West of the city center. His father,
originally from Tooting Bec, South of the River Thames in
London, had been working for the Publicis Advertising Agency
on the Champs-Élysées. Having met his mother, who at the
time was an Avon model from the Saône-et-Loire—and a client
of his—the two had moved in together on the left bank of the
River Seine, some eight kilometers from the hustle and bustle
of the city center in the bohemian, and artsy neighborhood.

As a result of his father's work, they had left the boulange-
rie-lined streets of that particular Parisian arrondissement
when he was a young child and had subsequently moved to the
quieter, more refined, middle-class suburbs of South London.
The grit and grime of Paris however had been intricately
woven into his fabric. He may well have attended one of the
top schools in England, but he also knew the side streets and
dark underbelly of Paris like only a true native can.

With his two laptops open in front of him, and a large glass of pastis in his hand, he tapped away at his keyboard, and with a flamboyant *'et voilà!'* finishing stroke, watched as his left screen downloaded an image of Franz Hagen. On the second screen to his right, he was re-reading a recent newspaper article from Le Monde on the Paris-based business tycoon Gabriel Sinclair. The same article that had prompted his move to the French capital.

Clicking through the various open tabs that he had been cross-referencing against the newspaper investments article— closely analyzing each irregular stock price and market spike that he suspected Sinclair had been associated with—he was slowly beginning to piece together the true motive behind his attempted murder, and sabotage, of the Allied Laboratories facility. He double-clicked on a previous investment article from the reputable Barron's weekly publication and confirmed what his gut was telling him. His mind was now clear. The confounding fog that had once loomed heavily above him had now lifted.

From under the tousled white sheets of his bed, an attractive long-haired brunette woman called out to him, the soft coffee-colored skin of her naked body silhouetted by the flickering of a large, slow-burning three-wicked candle.

"Cheri. Are you coming back to bed?" she asked in her best sultry, and seductive English.

"No," he replied. "I've got work to do."

"Mais cheri. Tu m'as promis!" she pouted, evidently disappointed with his priorities.

William hesitated for the briefest of moments and then finished his drink enthusiastically.

"Well in *that* case," he grinned, "how could I possibly refuse?"

With that, he stood up, stretched, and moved over to the bed beside her.

"Round three. Allons-y!"

CHAPTER TWELVE

FAILURE TO COMMUNICATE

THE NEXT MORNING, WITH A SPRING IN HIS STEP, AND with a broad satisfied smile slapped across his face, William Trevor Francis finished his morning espresso and exited the Starbucks café which overlooked the large mirrored office building he had been studying.

Crossing the Esplanade de La Défense, he wove his way between the many fountains and contemporary art sculptures dotted around the courtyard and entered the main lobby of the Areva skyscraper. Inside the large dark grey marble and polished steel lobby area he approached the front reception desk and asked to speak directly with Gabriel Sinclair of Sinclair Global Investments.

The young girl, dressed in an immaculately tailored Chanel ensemble, and wearing a beautifully simple, elegant, and sophisticated set of pearl earrings dutifully picked up her telephone and dialed the SGI office switchboard. A moment later she hung up and politely, but firmly, told him that a meeting with Mr. Sinclair would regrettably not be possible without an appointment. William wasn't going to take no for an answer. Looking directly into the overhead camera, which was pointed directly at him, he calmly insisted that Sinclair would most definitely want to see him, and politely asked the girl to dial the SGI office number once more.

"If you wouldn't mind trying again I'd appreciate it. You can tell that son of a bitch that William Trevor Francis is here for him."

The young girl picked up the phone and spoke into it a second time. She paused and asked him for his name once again.

"Francis. William Trevor Francis."

Moments later, two heavily set security guards entered the lobby and asked him to accompany them upstairs. Obligingly, he thanked the young receptionist for her help and followed the two formidable-looking guards around the corner, and into a private elevator. *Here we go* he thought to himself, mentally bracing for what he knew would be waiting for him. As soon as the elevator doors closed behind them, he was abruptly spun around and frisked. There was no standing on ceremony here. These guys knew what they were doing.

On the 14th floor, the elevator doors opened onto a large empty office space where Franz, dressed in a black single-breasted suit with a white dress shirt and dark grey tie, waited for him impatiently. He looked highly *bureaucratic,* William thought to himself. More accountant than assassin. On the other hand, the security guard standing next to him looked like an overstuffed piñata, ready to burst at the seams if hit too hard. William acknowledged the taser in his gorilla-esque hands. *Shit,* he thought to himself. *This piñata fights back!*

William quickly took stock of the deserted floor that appeared to be under renovation. Numerous heavy, opaque plastic tarps hung from the ceiling, presumably put in place to limit the amount of dust and debris being thrown about during the installation of the new drywall, electrics, and air ducting that littered the room floor. Counting Franz, his goon, and the two knuckleheads who had accompanied him up in the elevator, the odds were four to one. *Not great,* he thought. *But not impossible.* He took another look at the floor layout and addressed Franz directly.

"Where's Sinclair?"

Franz ignored the simple question.

"Is he clean?" he asked the two accompanying guards.

They both nodded in unison. He was clean. Franz signaled to the guard next to him and William was promptly tased squarely in the chest, the two men flanking him quickly taking a step back so as not to be shocked in the process. He dropped to the ground only to be kicked hard in the ribs. *Damn that hurts* he thought to himself, fighting away the pain that was now coursing through his muscles, splitting his head open like a lumberjack.

"Find out what he's doing here and then get rid of him. Call me when it's done," Franz barked at the three guards before walking out of the room, indifferent to their methods.

The three guards, obediently following orders like the well-trained stooges they were, man-handled William into a nearby chair, and firmly secured his hands behind his back.

"I'll kill you. I swear to God if it's the last thing I do I'll kill you all," he said—more of a promise than a threat.

The words had barely been uttered before he was tased again and punched, full force in the mouth, splitting his lips. Rocking backwards from the blow and toppling to the ground with a heavy thud, the chair creaked and groaned under the impact of the fall.

The guards hoisted the chair back onto its feet and continued.

"Now let's start again. Why are you here?"

"I told you. I'm here for Sinclair."

Another knuckle-sandwich to the face knocked his senses into next week. The guard chuckled at the severity of his punch, clearly impressed with himself. William shook his head and did his best to compartmentalize the pain. Grinning through a blood-soaked mouth he locked eyes with his opponent.

"What we've got here is a failure to communicate," he said, amused at the Cool Hand Luke reference he had just thought of.

"How's that for communication?" the guard said, hitting him hard in the guts.

William gritted his teeth and defiantly spat a mouthful of red-brown blood onto the floor and over the guard's black-laced shoes.

"Nope. Still not getting through. I'm afraid you're going to have to try harder," he said.

The second guard, waiting impatiently for his turn, stepped forward with the taser in his hands.

"Oh, I wouldn't worry about that. We're just warming up," he said, psychopathic delight in his threat.

Over the next fifteen minutes, William Trevor Francis endured what he would later consider '*a tough time*'. With his eyeballs almost popping out of their sockets and his muscles and joints seemingly ripping apart in uncontrollable spasms from the convulsion-inducing electric shocks he was being subjected to, he tried, unsuccessfully, to control and block the pain.

In the movies, this always looks like a piece of piss he thought to himself, imagining a Mel Gibson Lethal Weapon type of scenario in his head once a brief moment of clarity had slowly come back to him. *Damn those Hollywood guys. It's nothing like that! This bloody hurts!*

The chair rocked backwards and fell to the ground for a second time. Registering the weakness of the wooden frame he formulated a quick, desperate scenario to set himself free: *just a couple more falls should do it; just a couple more* but, to his total and utter dismay, it never happened.

"String him up," the third guard said, seemingly in control of that afternoon's office activities.

Untied from his chair and with the second guard holding the taser threateningly close to his neck, William was forcibly dragged, rebound, and strung up over the door, his arms pulled high above him by the second guard who was now pulling down forcibly on the other end of the rope.

William was now the piñata. *Bloody typical* he thought to himself. *The irony!*

"Go get the car and bring it round to the side entrance. This won't take long," the third guard said to his colleague as he clenched his fist and landed his first blow with the force and severity of a sledgehammer into the side of William's black and blue rib cage.

He was getting pummeled. A human punchbag. He knew there was no way he could endure much more of this. His insides were getting pulverized to a pulp.

"You're a strong bastard, I'll give you that."

William groaned. *Was that supposed to be a compliment?*

"Thanks?" he said, lifting his head as much as he could.

The guard, apparently tired of delivering his best Rocky Balboa performance, checked his bleeding knuckles and decided to go back to using the taser. William, still strung and hung tightly in place by the guard on the other side of the door, used the brief reprieve to spit another mouthful of blood onto the floor.

As William continued to get beat and shocked, the rope holding him in place over the top of the door slowly and imperceptibly began shifting, with each blow and jolt, towards the edge. With another merciless shock to his abdomen, the rope securing him in place finally slipped from the top of the door. He was free—albeit with his hands still firmly bound.

Like a tormented bull finally let loose in the ring, he charged the guard and without stopping, and with all the force he could muster, slammed him up against the wall. Using his knees, elbows, arms, and fists in a relentless barrage of attacks, he unleashed all of his pent-up hate and fury on the man—fighting for his life. Fighting for survival.

The second guard, slow to process what was happening, came running over to help his colleague but it was too late. William had hit his stride. He was now unstoppable. PCP was nothing compared to the fire of rage burning within him. Expertly rear-kicking the guard's knee and breaking his leg in a single blow, he spun around and, using the rope that was still binding his hands, straddled the screaming guard from behind, slowly strangling him to his well-deserved and timely death.

The third guard, regaining himself from his barrage of assault, launched at William who, with a limp body now on top of him was fumbling for the guard's gun—unable to reach it in time. The fight continued with each man now pushing and hurling the other up against the walls and desks, the plastic sheet-covered furniture smashing and crashing all around them.

The guard lunged and grabbed William around the throat, lifting him clear off the floor, strangling him in the process. Strung up like a chicken, his hands still bound, William tried with all his remaining might and resolve to break the stronghold but it wasn't working. He was coming up short and losing the battle. Turning blue in the face, the life literally being squeezed out of him like an orange, he desperately started stabbing his thumbs into the guard's eye sockets—pushing as hard as he could with all the remaining force left in his beaten body. The guard, blinded and screaming in pain released him, and William, seizing his moment, and with newfound adrenalin and resolve coursing through his veins, went back on the attack to finish off the job.

A jab to the right. A jab to the left. A left knee uppercut. A right knee uppercut and then, with an almighty push, he hurled the guard out of the office window, the office window glass smashing and shattering all around him. Weak on his legs, barely able to move and wincing from the pain that had taken over his entire body, he slowly retrieved the gun from the dead guard.

"I told you I'd kill you," he said matter-of-factly to the corpse lying on the floor in front of him.

Propping himself up on the desk he freed his bound wrists and checked the gun's magazine. As if on cue, the door flew open with the first guard having returned from the car. With lightning speed and precision, William slammed the magazine back into the grip, pulled back on the slide, swiveled, aimed, and fired a single shot—hitting the guard in the middle of his forehead. *Better than Bond* he thought to himself.

Staggering slowly away from the bloodbath in excruciating pain and discomfort, he opened the door to the main hallway and shuffled out into the corridor, his gun at the ready, on the hunt for Franz.

Running up the stairs, prompted by the sound of gunfire and with the peal of sirens clearly audible in the distance, a young security guard in his early 20's rounded the corner blocking his path.

"Halte ou je fais feu! Stop right there!" the young guard shouted, his voice trembling with fear and self-doubt.

William hesitated. The kid was young, inexperienced, and clearly out of his depth—not a real threat and probably poorly paid for the life-threatening predicament he now found himself in.

"My fight's not with you son. Don't be a hero," he said.

BANG! BANG! Two slugs buried themselves into the wall behind William. The kid, thankfully, was a lousy shot.

"Oi!" William shouted at him. "Knock it off!"

The kid hurried to take aim again.

BANG! A single round fired in return buried itself into the young security guard's leg—a flesh wound. He dropped to the ground, fear gripping him like a vice.

William approached, kicked the gun away, and crouched down beside him.

"I told you, my fight's not with you," and then continued to search the remainder of the floor.

Frustrated at finding the rest of the rooms empty he made his way back to the kid who was still bleeding and now crying in shock. Removing the kid's belt and baton, he quickly fashioned a makeshift tourniquet, grabbed the kid's hand, and held it in place over the gunshot wound.

"Where's the emergency exit?" he asked, knowing that he only had moments to spare before the police arrived.

Pointing towards the far left corner of the hallway, William hastily made his escape, disappearing down the stairwell and out into the side alley, triggering the building's fire alarm as he opened the door. With police cars now descending on the building, screeching to a halt with their sirens blaring, he expertly blended and disappeared into the crowd of confused employees and horrified passers-by who were all gathering, cell phones in hand, around the splattered body of the guard on the sidewalk.

CHAPTER THIRTEEN

MACCHIATO

MONIQUE LEFORT, DOING HER BEST SUPERMAN IMPER-sonation, was on the scene faster than a speeding bullet. She had been busy at her desk, filing reports, following up on leads, and monitoring her team's progress when the call about gunfire shots at La Défense had come in. Her gut, intuitively, had jumped to the foregone conclusion that her man was somehow, inexplicably involved. Grabbing her gun, badge, and a junior officer to drive her, she had arrived at the building's cordoned-off perimeter mere minutes after the building had been placed on lockdown.

She hated driving anywhere and actively avoided it whenever she could. In her opinion, the Paris public transportation network was so good, and usually so reliable, that the thought of owning and operating a car in the city center just seemed ludicrous. Plus Paris traffic was notoriously a bitch. No matter who you were, where you were going, or what you were driving, navigating the boulevards, avenues, or rues of Paris was a total nightmare. Don't even mention the périphérique!

She stepped out of her car, adjusted her jacket collar, gave instructions to her junior to grab her a caramel macchiato from the nearby Starbucks café, and approached the senior officer on duty. Flashing her credentials and introducing herself, she quickly got the lowdown on what they had determined so far.

"We've got one dead body under the tent over there with our coroner. Looks like he was pushed out of that window on the 14th floor and we have two more bodies inside, also on the 14th floor. One shot in the head and the other strangled. All of them male, Caucasian, in their 40's. So far it looks like they were all employed with SGI. My men are up there at the moment with forensics."

"SGI?" she asked. "As in Sinclair Global Investments?"

"Yup. The one and only."

"Anyone see anything? Any witnesses?" her interest and curiosity now definitely piqued.

"Well, we got one building security guard in the ambulance over there," he motioned with a nod of his head "young kid, shot in the leg but telling us everything we need to know, and a receptionist inside who's still talking to one of my guys."

"Thank you, Capitaine. Do you mind if I ask the guard a few questions myself? I think it might be related to a case I'm already working on."

"Go ahead. He's all yours," he said before leaving her alone, still waiting for her macchiato.

The young security officer, Jérôme Batiste, sat on a gurney with a bandage around his left thigh. The poor kid looked visibly distraught and Monique immediately sympathized with him. Wrong place, wrong time. Approaching him, she introduced herself, made sure he was comfortable, and then proceeded with her questions.

"So Jérôme, what can you tell me? Think back to the beginning. When did you first see the shooter? When did you first know that something was wrong?"

Jérôme looked up at her, still visibly distraught and in understandable shock at what he had just learned from a paramedic about the massacre on the 14th floor.

"When I heard gunshots. I was in the lobby, just doing my job making sure everyone was happy—observe and report—when I heard gunshots coming from upstairs," he said, trying his best to be as professional as possible under the circumstances.

"And then what happened? Once you heard gunfire?" she continued.

"I ran upstairs and called for help. No—I called for help when I heard screaming outside, then I hit the alarm, and *then* I ran upstairs."

"And then?" she asked.

"He shot me! I told him to stop and he said his fight wasn't with me—and then he shot me!"

"But only a flesh wound?" her tone now questioning what actually happened.

"It still bloody hurts. You try it!" the kid told her defiantly.

"No, I'm sure it does. But he didn't perceive you as a threat. He said *his fight wasn't with you?*"

"Yeah. He looked pretty beaten up. I don't know what they were doing up there, but he looked really bad. Like he'd really been roughed up."

"One last question. Who fired first? You or the suspect?"

The young guard hesitated. What was she insinuating? That he was somehow at fault here? Somehow *he* was to blame for getting shot?

"He did," he lied. "I told him to drop his weapon and he shot me. I fired my weapon in self-defense."

"OK. Let's get you taken care of and we can continue this at the hospital once you've been looked at."

With that, the young guard was rolled away and lifted into the back of an ambulance to get further medical attention. Monique, having finally been handed her coffee, sipped at the thick caramel-laced foam and pondered the facts. If William Trevor Francis had wanted to kill the kid he would have done so. But the flesh wound had been intentional. Why? Why let the kid go with a warning? And why bother with the tourniquet? To help him? It didn't make sense to her.

Back inside the building, video footage was being pulled from the security cameras and played back on the bank of security monitors. What was he doing? What did he want? Why was he being so brazen? she asked herself, genuinely perplexed by his behavior. And why was he going after Sinclair specifically? What was the connection?

"Get me everything you can. All cameras. All angles. Inside and out. And bring the receptionist in for questioning," she instructed a young female officer who had been diligently questioning other members of staff and employees in the lobby area.

"I want to go over her story again for myself. I'll clear everything with your Capitaine."

And with that, she walked back to her car and waited for her junior officer to drive her back to the office.

CHAPTER FOURTEEN

I THOUGHT WE WERE MATES?

Wearing his black leather jacket, dark blue boot-cut jeans, biker boots, and with his khaki military duffel bag slung over his back, William Trevor Francis shifted through the gears of his Suzuki 650 Dual Cross motorcycle, driving down from Paris to the South of France following the road signs to Marseille. Day gradually turned to night as he slowly chipped away at the kilometers of tarmac in the hope of seeking out help from an old army buddy that he had served with in the same regiment.

Pulling off in the Bonneveine neighborhood adjacent to the Parc Borély, William whipped his bike down Avenue de la Serane and drove down to the bottom of the quiet residential cul-de-sac. Tired, thirsty, and sore, he pulled up to the large metal gate of his trusted mate's family home and rang the buzzer. A young, pretty girl in her teens and wearing a pink floral print dress approached him at the main gate followed by her father, a black, handsome Apollo Creed-type man who looked great and had obviously done well for himself.

"Salut mon ami. Il y a longtemps qu'on ne s'est pas vu" William said, genuine pleasure in his voice.

"Too long my friend!" Luc replied. "I've seen you on TV. You look terrible!"

"Ha! So I've been told. And who's this lovely young lady?"

"My daughter Sophie. She's grown a bit since you last saw her," Luc chuckled.

"Yes she has. What are you now? Thirteen? Fourteen?"

"Fourteen," she beamed.

Luc looked at his daughter with pride.

"Why don't you come in Will? Audrey's inside. She'd love to see you. How long's it been? Ten, twelve years?"

"Something like that. I can't keep count these days. I'm getting old!"

The two men laughed and gave each other a manly hug and pat on the back.

"Beer?" Luc asked.

"Absolutely mon ami. Abso-bloody-lutely!"

Sipping a cold Kronenbourg on the back porch, the two men reminisced about old the times, their service together, and their mishaps along the way. Fun times all around. Even when they thought the world was going to Hell, the two men had been inseparable. True brothers from a different mother!

Black and white; salt and pepper, yin and yang, these two men had always had each other's back.

Luc's wife, a strikingly elegant and sophisticated woman from Mauritius, brought out a tray of amuse-bouche from the kitchen.

"What have you been doing? You don't look too good," she said to William who was smiling, admiringly, at her.

The two had nearly hit it off some twenty years ago when he and Luc—on weekend leave from the regiment—had been strutting the Biarritz and St-Jean-de-Luz coastline, checking out its nightlife and chatting up the young and beautiful tourists that vacationed there. William Trevor Francis, handsome and fearless, had seen the young Audrey in a discothèque opposite the Plage du Miramar, but it had been Luc, 'the quiet one', that had taken her home that night. Ever since then, and to William's great pleasure, the two lovebirds had been inseparable.

"Love you too ma chère."

Audrey rolled her eyes and disappeared back into the kitchen to let the two men talk privately.

"You've done well for yourself mate. How the Hell can you afford all of this? You rob a bank or something?"

"That's your style, not mine. So what's with the unexpected visit?" he replied.

William finished his beer and, using his lighter against the padded flesh of his left hand, popped the cap off a fresh cold one.

"I need your help mate. I'm in way over my head."

Explaining the long sequence of events that had led him here, starting with Vinny and ending with Sinclair, he recounted as much as he could in the hopes that his pal could shed some light on his predicament. Divulging that he now believed 'the job' was never about stealing a formula and hijacking research files for a competitor, but that it was, he suspected, about stopping a pharmaceutical company from making a major breakthrough and shorting its stock value, he turned to Luc for answers.

"What do you think?" he asked, popping the cap off yet another beer.

"About what? Industrial sabotage? You think this billionaire is stopping a medical breakthrough in order to cash in? Betting on a competitor's success? I don't buy it."

"Why not? It's not like I haven't been paid to do similar jobs in the past. I've done tons of corporate gigs just like this one! Whether the stocks go up or down makes no difference as long as you're betting on the right outcome. And for all I know, the bastard got away with whatever he was after before the place even blew up!"

Luc paused, reflected for a moment, and continued.

"And you think he'd commit murder and frame you for it in order to maximize his profits?"

William picked up his smokes from the table, lit one up, and mulled over the credibility of what he was actually insinuating. He was on his fifth beer and his mind was racing.

"Yes!" he said, decisively, slamming his beer bottle on the table. "Why not? This is industrial sabotage and I'm the perfect scapegoat to pin it on."

He continued to count out the facts on his fingers.

"An international thief who was supposed to have died in the explosion. I'm an easy target. He invests on a loss over here, invests in a competitor doing well over there—it all adds up! Why else would there be photos of me at the lab? I was framed!"

Luc listened intently, trying to make sense of it all. He shook his head.

"You want something stronger? Calvados?" he asked.

William winked. "I thought you'd never ask!"

Sipping on the dark amber spirit, enjoying the warm glow of the apple brandy, he popped another cheese-filled vol-au-vent into his mouth.

"You ever come across the name Franz Hagen? Anything back in the service maybe?" he asked.

"No. Never heard of him."

Inside the kitchen, Audrey, eavesdropping on the conversation, held her breath and continued listening intently.

"I don't know what you're involved in—and I don't want to know—but whatever you need you can count on me for help," Luc added.

"I know. Thanks, man! Just being able to lie low while I do some digging around is more that I could hope for."

"Anytime." Luc stood up. "It's late and I promised Audrey I'd help her with some errands in the morning. Make yourself at home. I'll ask her to make up the spare room for you."

William poured himself another 3 finger measure drink, lit up another smoke, and smiled.

"Merci mon ami! I appreciate it!"

"You want to go shooting tomorrow? It's rabbit season. Might be good for walking off that hangover you're going to have," Luc continued. He nodded towards the bottle. "That stuff'll kill you."

William groaned. "The way things have been going recently I'm not sure I even *want* to wake up in the morning."

Raising his glass in the air to Luc he cheered. "Sans crainte ..."

Luc finished off their army war cry, "... Sans regrets" and turned to join his wife.

Inside the kitchen and with William still outside on the porch drinking and smoking himself into an early grave, Audrey confronted her husband with concern in her voice.

"I heard you on the phone last night. Why didn't you tell him the truth? Why did you tell him you didn't know that man?"

For the first time in a *very* long time, a flash of fury took over him.

"Keep it down and stay out of my affairs," Luc threatened her, the tone in his voice forceful and unambiguous.

EARLY THE NEXT MORNING, AUDREY WOKE HER COMA-tosed houseguest with a large cup of coffee and a plate of freshly baked croissants. She carefully placed the coffee and pastries on the table next to him and handed him a bottle of headache pills as he stirred from his drunken slumber.

"I thought you might need these," she said, handing him the pills. "You haven't changed a bit!"

William groaned, grinned, and slowly pulled himself upright.

"Audrey, you're a lifesaver. Merci!"

Unscrewing the bottle with a hangover-induced tremor in his hands, he shook out a small handful of red pills and swallowed them down, praying to the gods that he wouldn't have to suffer too long before they kicked in.

LATER THAT MORNING, LUC AND WILLIAM WERE BOTH out reminiscing again whilst ambling through the exquisite pine-laden forests of the Callelongue, on the outskirts of Marseille. William had no intention of firing his gun or killing anything but, with his shotgun slung over his arm, he was definitely enjoying the exercise, the fresh air, the sun-scorched countryside, and the breathtakingly beautiful vantage point overlooking the dark blue Mediterranean waters in the distance. *It doesn't get much better than this* he thought to himself. He turned to Luc who was a couple of paces to his left.

"Why didn't you tell me the truth yesterday about knowing Franz?"

"What are you talking about?" Luc replied defensively.

"Mate. I might be getting on a bit, but I'm not deaf. I overheard you and Audrey talking in the kitchen."

Luc stopped dead in his tracks, his stunningly ornate Parallelo 12 gauge shotgun now trained on his former buddy.

"You should never have come here," he said. A blend of annoyance and indignation in his tone.

"What are you talking about? I came to you for help! After all this time this is what you're doing? This is how it's going down?"

"Pull the cartridges out and throw them on the ground. Turn around and start walking."

William had no choice but to do what he was told. *Shit,* he thought to himself. *Can't I just get a break?*

"Why are you doing this? What's in it for you?" he asked, genuinely trying to understand Luc's irrational motives.

"I've got a family to support and there's a hefty price tag on your head. This lifestyle doesn't come cheap."

"And you'd sell me out for it? I thought we were mates?"

"I hear Vinny was killed at his club. Are you responsible for that?"

"Don't be a bloody idiot. Of course not. I came to you for help!"

"Yes. And by doing so you put my family in danger."

"It doesn't have to be this way, Luc. We can fix this. It's not too late."

"Franz knew you would come here. He's been one step ahead of you the whole time. You're not as good as you think you are. You led the wolf right to my door."

"So how do you know him? Were you and Vinny involved with Victor? Setting up side deals? Running guns? Enlighten me. Is that the connection to Franz?"

"It's a smaller world than you think."

"Luc. Trust me. You don't want to do this. We can still make it right. You and me, like the old days."

"The old days are long gone, Will. Now walk!"

As they continued to walk, Luc's phone rang. He grabbed it and answered the call.

"Yes. He's with me now, just like you said. We're on our way there."

Arriving at a small abandoned hunter's cabin hidden from view by the pine and juniper-filled tree line, Luc removed a small roll of duct tape from his inside jacket pocket.

"Turn around with your hands behind your back. You know the drill."

Placing the tip of his barrel against the nape of William's neck, he fumbled with his left hand to secure the binding.

"Don't try anything smart," he said, frustrated at not being able to manipulate the tape more easily with one hand.

"Now why on earth would I do that?"

Sensing a moment of weakness and a perceived lapse in

concentration, William pushed back obstinately against the twin barrels in his nape and then immediately pulled forward and to the side, throwing Luc off balance, the shotgun's blued-steel barrels lunging unsteadily into the air. With a reverse kick to the knee and then a parry of leg blows and head butts, he managed to knock Luc, momentarily dazed and disarmed, to the ground. With his hands still bound behind his back, he fumbled frantically with a small 4" pocket knife that he had noticed was sitting on a ledge by the side window. Free at last, he took a step back as Luc, now back on his feet and with his clenched fists raised, readied himself. The fight was on.

As the two men squared off against each other, each one waiting for the other to make the first move, William gave his old friend one last chance to back down.

"You sure you want to do this? You really think you've got a chance against me?"

"You're old and you're out of shape. You're not as good as you think you are. You never were."

"Fuck you—I've never been better." William quipped back, lying through his teeth. "Bring it on."

Burying the rusty blade into the wooden floor with a decisive flick of his hand, the two men skirted the narrow confines of the wooden shack, circling the dust-covered floor, each man weighing up the other. Expertly throwing punches, jabs, and kicks—each man outmaneuvering the other—this was a pure test of skill, endurance, and willpower.

As the two men continued to hurl each other up against the walls and onto the floor, demolishing the inside of the ramshackle cabin in the process, William, finally able to secure Luc in a leg hold on the floor, slowly applied pressure to Luc's neck which was now trapped behind his knee. Witnessing the life slowly draining out of him, he released his suffocating grip before it was too late, leaving Luc to gasp helplessly on the floor next to him.

"For Audrey and Sophie's sake, I'm going to let you live. But now you're going to do exactly what I say."

Getting slowly to his feet William crossed the cabin to pick up the shotgun that was lying on the floor, but in the split second that he had taken his eyes off of his opponent, Luc had managed to grab the rusty knife and charge him. With one deflective swipe, and with a sharp twisting of the wrists, William turned the blade away from himself and onto Luc, who with the sheer force of momentum behind him, impaled himself in the chest. Looking Luc directly in the eyes, William buried the blade home for good measure.

"This is on you, my friend. This is your own fault."

Watching Luc's lifeless body slowly sag and drop to the ground he composed himself, checked outside the cabin to make sure that he was alone, and then retrieved the knife and the shotgun. Flipping Luc's body over, he removed his cell phone and stepped outside for a smoke to gather his thoughts. What a morning! What a goddamn awful bloody morning!

––––––––––––

As dusk fell to the captivating sound of cicadas, William Trevor Francis was alerted to the quiet rumble of a car approaching in the distance. Crouching down behind the base of a large tree, the small abandoned hunter's cabin only twenty meters in front of him, he watched and waited from the shadows as the car approached and parked in a cloud of heavy dust. A man stepped out of the black Jaguar, gun in hand. William recognized him immediately from the SGI building. It was Franz.

Carefully scanning the outside perimeter for signs of Luc, Franz cautiously entered the cabin and immediately saw the motionless body on the floor. Arms and legs bound. A burlap sack covering its head. Approaching it, he knelt down and pulled back the hood, only to reveal Luc's expressionless face. Immediately aware of the trap he was in he spun around to face his attacker, but it was too late. With an almighty blow to his face with the butt of the Italian-made shotgun, William immediately and ruthlessly rendered him immobile.

Taking his gun and leading him out at gunpoint to his car, he frisked Franz for any concealed weapons, popped the trunk, and ordered him in.

"Now let's you and me finish this once and for all," he said.

Franz, more amused than concerned at how the tables had been turned, smiled with indifference.

"You have no idea what you're doing."

"Shut up and get in!" William ordered, delivering a second heavy blow to his face, knocking him out stone cold.

Pulling Franz's jacket down and securing his arms as best as he could, William shoved a dirty cloth into Franz's mouth and closed the trunk. Getting into the driver's seat he tapped on the center console's navigation display and pulled up the most current driving directions, the 'departing from' location flashing on the screen.

William couldn't help but laugh to himself. Finally, something was going his way. Hitting the 'return to' button he started the ignition and floored the gas. *Well, that was easy!* he thought to himself. *About time I caught a break!*

CHAPTER FIFTEEN

BLACK TIES AND BULLETS

TWO DAYS LATER FOLLOWING THE DISCOVERY OF LUC'S dead body in the hunter's cabin on the outskirts of Marseille, forensics teams were analyzing the cold stiffened corpse, and lifting tire tread impressions from the tracks imprinted in the soft soil.

Audrey, having first notified the police of the disappearance of her husband when he hadn't returned home two nights earlier with an old army friend, had driven herself to the crime scene as soon as she had heard about the gruesome discovery. It was a small neighborhood and bad news traveled fast. Unable to keep her away from the scene, she had identified the puffy blue-black body of her husband and was now being consoled by a junior officer.

As Luc's body was tagged, bagged, and loaded into the back of an ambulance, the police continued to take down all the necessary details they could gather from her and the local huntsman who, with his two golden retrievers, had uncovered the unfortunate victim.

LATER THAT DAY, BACK AT THE LOCAL POLICE STATION, information was slowly being uploaded onto the main district server.

Monique Lefort's case file on William Trevor Francis was now getting even bigger. Sitting in her small grey 12x12 Paris office, a large bottle of Badoit and a 'jambon-beurre' sandwich on her desk, she stared at the wall in front of her, slowly piecing together and deciphering this new information. Taking a large bite of her sandwich, she got up and added a photo of Luc's body to her wall collage, sticking it firmly in place with a thumbtack. This guy was leaving a bloodbath behind him. *But why?*

Mentally absorbing the facts in front of her, she played out the scenario that made the most logical sense. The first victim, Marie Boyer, dead at the lab in Budapest; the rooftop chase at the Ritz-Carlton; the ensuing car chase; the sighting of her man by a gas station attendant on the outskirts of Brno; the murder of Vinny Menard at his strip club in Berlin; the killing of three notorious gang members in a café on the outskirts of Berlin; the mayhem that had ensued at the corporate offices of SGI, resulting in the further death of three men and the injury of a fourth. And now, unbelievably, another victim in the South of France of someone, who his wife had claimed, was a close friend and confidant. She stared at the single photo of William Trevor Francis that was pinned to the middle of her wall, the one solid connection between all of the incidents. *What the Hell is going on?* she thought to herself. *What the Hell is he up to?*

ON THE OUTSKIRTS OF THE BOIS DE BOULOGNE TO THE West of the Paris city center and only a short 20-minute drive from La Défense and the SGI offices, William was now parked a ways back outside of a huge mansion, the strikingly elegant and iconic Eiffel Tower illuminated in the distance. The frenzied barking of dogs could be heard from within the compound walls as he observed a number of high-end luxury cars arrive at the residence, passing through the gates only once they had been cleared by security. Taking one last, long drag of his cigarette, he stubbed it out and started the Jaguar's engine.

Driving slowly in front of the main gates, paying particular attention to the many armed guards on duty, he turned onto a deserted side road and parked his car out of sight. Satisfied that the car was sufficiently well hidden from the main road, he grabbed the small set of binoculars from his bag and climbed a nearby tree to better observe the complex and its activities. Settling into a suitable position, he looked at his watch. It was 7:32 pm.

In the hubbub of black ties and ballgowns now arriving en masse, he spotted the individual he was targeting next: Gabriel Sinclair, the owner of the house and the host for that evening. The place, he thought to himself, resembled Fort Knox with its armed guards, dogs, surveillance cameras, and floodlights. He would have to think outside of the box on this one. He would need to improvise. He checked his watch again. 8:46 pm. Time to get going. No time like the present. As he descended the tree and returned to his car, he heard a muffled banging and scraping coming from inside the trunk. Popping it open, he immediately landed a right hook onto Franz's jaw, knocking him out, again.

"I said shut up!"

Grabbing his harness and grappling hook from his bag, he double-checked his equipment, verified his bindings, and walked over to the large, ivy-clad, 12-foot brick wall.

Outside of Sinclair's main residence, two guards, each with FAMAS 5.56 assault rifles hanging from their shoulders met under the glare of one of the main building floodlights and shared a few words over a cigarette. In the background, only twenty meters away and under cover of the dark shadows being cast by the full moon, William carefully climbed up and over the perimeter wall. Descending into the complex, he saw the two men and immediately froze, dangling in mid-air, his grappling hook and harness straining under his weight.

Slowly, carefully, he lowered himself down into the dark vegetation below. With his eyes still firmly locked on the two men, he followed them as they separated and continued with their respective rounds. With the stealth of a Bengal tiger, he proceeded along the inner rim of the wall, using its foliage as cover, and made a hasty dash across the vast expanse of lawn, rolling beneath the undercarriage of a new Bentley Continental GT, one of the many luxury cars now parked on the gravel outside. Loud music and laughter resonated in the background. The guests were evidently enjoying a splendid evening!

Lying on his back in the cold, sharp, and angular bed of gravel, William saw the bottom of the main doors open and two young adults, a man, and a woman, leaving the mansion party past the guardsman. Stumbling through the row of parked cars, a bottle of Ruinart champagne and two champagne flutes in their hands, the two lovebirds kissed their way over to his set of wheels. In fits of laughter, the young Romeo carelessly set the bottle of bubbles and his two glasses on the hood of his Storm Grey Mulliner, a fine moose of white foam ejecting from the top of the bottle onto the pristine piano-finished paintwork. Giggling and kissing, like school kids in the back of a bus, she unzipped his black satin-lined trousers and pushed him backwards into the open rear passenger side door, falling on top of him in a hot and horny mess.

Underneath the vehicle, still sandwiched between the courtyard gravel and the undercarriage of the Bentley, William was growing impatient.

"Screw this," he muttered under his breath. "Just get on with it."

Biding his time and cursing profusely under his breath, he waited, impatiently, for the next burst of excited and sexually charged giggles before rolling out from underneath the car's belly. Swiping the expensive bottle of champagne and the two glasses that were still on the hood of the car he headed towards the main building entrance, quickly formulating a plan in his head.

Feigning a drunken stupor and sipping straight from the bottle, he staggered around to the building's main entrance and up the main staircase towards the guardsman at the top. *Alright Will, you got this* he told himself as the guard, as a matter of precaution and routine, asked to see his invitation.

With his hands full, William smiled, fumbled, and muttered incoherently, forcing the guard who was struggling to understand him to lean in closer. In a split second, William seized the opportunity and clocked the heavy champagne bottle over his head, instantly knocking the guard out. With an almighty heave, he pushed the guard up and over the stairwell and down into the dark abyss of bushes below—tossing the two glasses and the bottle after him for good measure. *Easy come easy go.*

Preparing himself for Phase Two, he opened the heavy oak doors and entered the building and the main lobby which was now heaving with invitees. Discreetly, and as inconspicuously as possible, he made his way up the central stairway towards the first floor. *So far so good* he thought to himself, pleased that he hadn't been caught yet.

———

OUTSIDE, BACK IN THE WOODS AND OBSCURED BY THE dark cover of trees, a loud banging and thumping could be heard coming from the trunk of the black Jaguar. Inside the vehicle, a sharp metal bar—part of the spare tire jack—ripped through the mocha leather stitched back seats. A balled and bleeding fist squeezed its way between the metal seat springs and the soft padded upholstery, tearing a hole big enough for an arm, a shoulder, and a head. The backseat was giving birth, only not to a beautiful, bouncing baby boy. No. The backseat was giving birth to a bloodied and thoroughly pissed-off 56-year-old Austrian madman.

Franz, now squeezing and dragging his body through the cushioned cavity like a creature from Aliens collapsed onto the rear bench seat. Collecting his senses, he exited the car, checked his surroundings, and headed on foot towards the main house, alerting the guards at the perimeter gates as soon as he approached them.

In the main residence, William had quickly located Sinclair's office on the first floor and was hastily opening drawers, cabinets, and files trying to find anything out of the ordinary. Anything that would incriminate Sinclair. Scouting the room and studying the various paintings hanging on the wall, he went over to the one that had grabbed his interest. Carefully placing the antique painting depicting the Battle of Agincourt on the floor he looked at the wall safe that was hidden behind it.

"Bollocks!" he muttered in anger and frustration. If only he had his bloody tools with him!

Frustrated but undeterred, he grabbed the Glock from his waistband and walked out of the office. He'd confront Sinclair face-on! As he crossed to the balcony he heard the loud commotion coming from below. A single shot was fired, shattering the intricately carved mahogany banister in front of him.

Armed security guards were now firing towards him, a barrage of bullets raining down around him as the guests fled the commotion in a chaotic stampede of black ties and bullets.

Downstairs, a bloodied and disheveled Franz was hurriedly advising Sinclair to leave the premises as quickly as possible.

"You should get to the airfield straight away. I'll stay here and deal with him," he told his boss, his bloodshot red eyes filled with seething rage.

From the upstairs window, William could see Sinclair being ushered into a car. *He was getting away!* Smashing the diamond-shaped window panes with the muzzle of his gun, he fired off as many shots as he could. A few rounds made their way into the car's body—but unfortunately, none of the bullets hit the body of their intended target. With the sound of guards now running up the stairs towards him, he had no choice but to watch Sinclair escape.

As Sinclair's bullet-riddled Maybach roared past the security guards and out through the main gates onto Boulevard Lannes, Sinclair reached into his pocket and retrieved his phone.

"Get my plane ready for Zürich. I'll be there in 30 minutes!"

William was trapped, heavy gunfire now coming relentlessly his way as he watched Sinclair's car drive off down the driveway, disappearing through the gates and around the corner. With the all too familiar sound of sirens approaching the property, he checked his magazine. Only one round remaining. With the guards now nearing the top of the stairs and their bullets getting closer to him he didn't stand a chance against them. Taking a deep breath, he fired off his last slug towards the stairwell and jumped out of the window onto the ground below. It was a long fall—and it hurt. A lot.

Panic-stricken guests were still frantically trying to leave the property, desperately running towards their cars and scrambling for their keys that the valet service, in the commotion, had left unattended. With gunfire still going off inside the main house, the first police cars to arrive at the scene remained cautiously parked outside the driveway entrance, quickly taking stock of the situation and calling for immediate backup.

William, reeling on the ground from a fall that he would usually have taken in his stride, refused to let the pain in his legs get the better of him. Without wasting any further time he got to his feet, staggered over to the valet station, and grabbed the keys to the midnight-blue Jaguar F Type that was parked closest to him. Punching the ignition button, he floored the pedal, spitting a hail of gravel through the windows of the downstairs cloakroom.

With a new round of bullets hailing down on him from the upstairs windows he fish-tailed over the damp grass and went, flat out, towards the exit. Expertly throwing the car around the tight corners of the beautifully manicured forecourt, he skillfully avoided the finely attired guests and instead made a B-line for the guards who were now firing at him from the front. With alarm bells shrilling from across the grounds he accelerated as the gates in front of him began to close.

A fearlessly stupid guard tried to stand in front of the gates, firing at the car as it approached but jumped out of the way at the last second as William smashed his way through, past the line of parked police vehicles, and out onto the long, dark and lonely road. The rear lights of Sinclair's car barely visible in the distance.

Back at the mansion, Franz was also preparing to give chase. Having seen his adversary take off, he summoned two groups of men to their vehicles.

"I'll be in the first car. Second team, you follow," he barked, slamming the door and cocking his gun.

This was war.

CHAPTER SIXTEEN
ON YOUR KNEES!

THE POLICE RADIO ON MONIQUE'S DESK CRACKLED TO life, spitting out updates of a high-speed chase and shoot-out through the bourgeois-filled boulevards adjacent to the Bois-de-Boulogne. Working late again at the office, she immediately put down her dish of Vietnamese Bún Thang chicken noodles and ran into her Capitaine's office. Empty! Skidding along the deserted corridors she wondered briefly if she was the only one working that night at the station. *One day I really must get a life* she told herself. Grabbing the keys to her car, and unable to find an available officer to accompany her, she resigned herself to the fact that she would have to drive to the scene alone. She knew it was him. She knew with absolute certainty that her man was involved! The only thing she wasn't certain of anymore was whether William Trevor Francis was her *only* suspect. The repeated involvement of Gabriel Sinclair, and William Trevor Francis's high-profile presence at his offices, didn't make sense to her.

Monitoring the Bourne Supremacy-esque chase over the

car radio she threw her police Renault Mégane into drive and floored the gas, hitting the street with a heavy thud as she over-corrected and leveled out her car. She was going to catch him!

WILLIAM, COMFORTABLY BEHIND THE WHEEL OF HIS F Type, and now throwing the car around like a Formula 1 pro, continued to give chase through the narrow streets of the swanky 16th arrondissement, slowly gaining ground on Sinclair's car ahead. Behind him, Franz and his supporting vehicle were both gaining. Leaning out of the passenger side window, one of Franz's men fired at William, forcing him to duck and swerve to avoid the hail of bullets coming his way. Continuing to give chase through the smaller neighborhood roads and up onto the larger Boulevard des Maréchaux towards the périphérique, William, now with an entourage of police vehicles behind him, continued relentlessly to give chase to the Maybach ahead.

Driving his accelerator into the floorboards and swerving between the late evening traffic on the circular ring road encasing the city center, he did his best Lewis Hamilton impersonation and started overtaking the cars on his left and right, all the while dodging and weaving the gunfire coming his way, desperately trying to catch up with Sinclair who was now comfortably out in front.

Speeding ahead, Sinclair's driver managed to swerve hard and successfully pulled off the freeway exit ramp at the last minute, leaving William stuck on the wrong side of a large commercial freight truck. Desperately wanting to take the same exit, but with his window of opportunity flashing past, he decided he had no choice but to gamble with his life. Swerving wide to the left and then driving his car clear under the belly of the truck to the right, he managed to make it through to the other side, ducking his head just in time as the car's roof clipped the undercarriage of the truck and was ripped off like a tin of beans.

Plowing into the green and white reflective barricades at the mouth of the freeway exit, he desperately tried to correct his car as it swerved and fishtailed before crashing hard into the right-hand side barrier and over the lip of the shoulder— his two front tires bursting like balloons as he screeched and skidded to an abrupt standstill.

"Shit!" he yelled, furious with himself and his recklessness. "Shit! Shit! Shit!"

Franz and the other vehicle, both unable and unwilling to attempt the same outrageous kamikaze maneuver, had no choice but to pass William's battered and smoking wheels, stopping a short way up on the hard shoulder ahead. As the men ran out of their vehicles, they started firing again in his direction, the other cars on the périphérique swerving, accelerating, and avoiding the Tarantino-esque scene with utter terror and panic.

Stunned, but miraculously not seriously injured, William managed to shove his car into reverse and slowly drove his wreck—the two front rims sparking like Catherine wheel fireworks—away from the gunfire and the apocalyptic mayhem. He floored the gas once more, his front wheels cutting deep grooves into the road's surface as he continued, persistently, with his pursuit.

Franz and his men jumped back into their cars, reversed down the hard shoulder, and rocketed down the off-ramp after their incapacitated prey, who was now sputtering through the quiet industrial section of town towards the Grand Parc des Docks de Saint-Ouen. Sinclair's car was nowhere to be seen. Sinclair had evaded him. Sinclair had won.

As William's car slowly limped along the quiet, deserted side road, Franz and the second car closed in on their compromised target. A string of police cars rounded the corner and an overhead helicopter now joined the chase. To his right, William saw the battered road sign to the local airport only 2 kilometers away. *Yes!* he thought to himself. He still had a fighting chance!

Driving through the small airport's perimeter fence, past the security guard manning his booth, and onto the black tarmac where his Learjet and pilot were waiting for him, Sinclair jumped out of his car, ran up the flight of steps, and yelled frantically at his pilot.

"Get us out of here. NOW!"

Smashing through the barricade and screeching onto the runway, William Trevor Francis, determined in his dogged pursuit, veered along the asphalt after Sinclair, who was now taxiing and preparing for take-off. In the cockpit, the pilot scrambled desperately to get his final checks and approvals completed before the tower, once alerted to the ensuing chaos below, would shut them down.

William's car continued to moan and groan, heaving its last petroleum-fueled sigh before finally packing up halfway down the runway with a procession of police cars in pursuit, as Sinclair's jet slowly picked up speed and took off into the cold night Parisian sky and out of the country.

Franz and his men, still in their cars, watched from the airport perimeter chain-linked fence as their boss tucked his wheels and disappeared into the blanket of darkness that had descended upon them.

William was now surrounded and trapped like a caged animal by an army of armed police. Satisfied that there was nothing more they could do at this stage, Franz and his men drove off in silence. They had lost the battle, but the war was far from over.

———

ARRIVING AT THE AIRPORT, MONIQUE LEFORT WAS ON the scene just in time to witness the Learjet take off, and William being ordered out of his car at gunpoint.

"Get out of the vehicle and place your hands behind your head. Now!" the police officer yelled, his 92FS aimed unequivocally at William's temple.

As Monique hastily stepped out of her car, William obligingly did as he was instructed.

"On your knees!" the police officer continued.

William dutifully got down onto his knees as a second police officer, with handcuffs, stepped in.

With his hands now firmly secured behind his back, he was unceremoniously pushed forward and off-balance, slamming his face against the hard cold ground. With anger and hatred in his eyes, he watched the beacon of lights from Sinclair's plane gradually disappear and fade out of sight.

It was all over. At least for now.

CHAPTER SEVENTEEN

YOUR ARSE IS MINE

AT THE DOWNTOWN POLICE STATION THE NEXT MORN-ing, William Trevor Francis, unwashed, unkempt, and look-ing very much worse for wear was being questioned in stark contrast by an immaculately dressed, beautifully styled, and remarkably composed Monique Lefort. Placing her café au lait and morning croissant aux amandes on the table in front of her, she signaled to the two armed officers to take a step back and sat down at the seat across from her suspect who was sit-ting patiently, chained by his wrists and ankles to the concrete floor.

"I know there's more to this than you're giving me. I'm not sure if you were responsible for the explosion at the Allied Laboratories and I don't know if you had any involvement with Marie Boyer's death, but I do know that I'm not going to let you run around the country on a shooting spree! This needs to stop now!"

"You have your ways and I have mine," he responded po-litely, but matter of factly.

"No. You do things *my* way now. *I'm* in charge here," she shot back with confidence and conviction. *Who the Hell does this guy think he is?* she asked herself.

William smiled and nodded. He liked this woman. *Who the Hell is she and where the Hell did she come from?*

Monique continued. "Now tell me. What's your connection with Sinclair? How is he involved in all of this?"

William looked at her inquisitively. He was impressed but remained silent. He wasn't going to give anything up that easily. The last thing he needed was more badges running around the countryside, complicating matters for him. The more suits that got involved, the less chance he had of getting to Sinclair. And that was his mission: getting Sinclair.

"I've got nine dead bodies in the morgue—all of them leading back to you. If you don't start fully cooperating with me, I'm going to throw the book at you and watch you rot in jail. I don't care if you're innocent or not. Do you understand? Am I making myself perfectly clear?" she continued.

William was captivated by this woman and her passion— impressed with her forthright attitude. *Oh, this girl's terrific,* he thought to himself. *Absolute dynamite!*

After a reflective moment, he acknowledged her question. "This is my fight. You're only going to slow me down."

"No, I won't slow you down, I'll lock you up!" she told him before grabbing her coffee and pastry and getting up. "This is my show, not yours. You'd be wise to remember that."

OUTSIDE ON A QUIET TREE-LINED SIDE STREET, SITTING patiently in his car waiting for updates, Franz hung up his phone with one of the junior officers working at the DRI offices, a young junior officer who had recently been added to Franz's payroll. He paused, and then dialed another number, reporting back to Sinclair.

"I've just been told they still have him in custody. He's not giving them much, but they have enough to hold him. They'll be transferring him in a few days."

There was a brief moment of silence before Sinclair spoke on the other end.

"Make sure he doesn't get there. Do whatever it takes."

———————

TWO DAYS LATER, WILLIAM TREVOR FRANCIS WAS IN THE back of a Renault police van being driven through the outskirts of town to an alternate location. The high-profile nature of the handsome 'Thomas Crown Affair' Englishman in French custody had been garnering an unusual amount of international media coverage and police officials, as well as the city Mayor, were now concerned with the safety and security of their suspect. As such, a more secure locale had been deemed a sensible precautionary move.

William, sitting in the back of the van with his ankles and wrists cuffed to a heavy chain secured to the floor, fumbled in his top pocket for his cigarettes, his movement severely restricted by his bindings. The two armed guards opposite him looked on, watching him wrestle with his shackles.

"No smoking!" one of them said finally.

"Seriously? You've literally been watching me struggle here for 5 minutes!"

"C'est interdit!" said the second one.

"Give me a break! I was specifically told I could keep them. What you going to do? Arrest me?" he said flippantly, putting a smoke between his lips. He rummaged again in his top pocket. *Bollocks! They kept my lighter.* Leaning forward towards the guards he asked for a light, already knowing what the answer would be.

The guards looked at him incredulously before both, simultaneously responding "Non!"

All of a sudden and seemingly out of nowhere, the escorting police cars at the front and rear of the van were simultaneously T-boned, catapulting both cars into the air and into the middle of the busy Rue Saint Lazare intersection of the 9th quarter, finally rolling to a standstill on the footsteps of the ornate 17th century Eglise de la Sainte Trinité Catholic church.

The police van driver, having witnessed what had just happened in front of him, immediately slammed on his brakes, knocking William, and the two guards in the back, off-balance. In the split second that the van was stationary, it too was rammed by a large truck on the left, propelling it twenty meters to the right, where it eventually skidded to an abrupt halt on its side.

Monique Lefort, trailing behind the convoy in a fourth vehicle, driven by her senior officer Capitaine Kristoff, stared in sheer bewilderment as total chaos erupted around them. With pedestrians, vendors and tourists all screaming and fleeing for safety, panic fell on the busy intersection like a dirty bomb.

William, knocked to the floor by the impact, slowly shook his head and came to his senses. With a disco ball of flashing lights in front of his eyes and a searing pain shooting down his neck and into his shoulders, he assessed his wounds before quickly helping the guard who was lying on the floor next to him. Seriously injured but coherent, he gave him a reassuring pat on the shoulder. He'd be fine. However, the other guard in the back with them had been knocked unconscious, a small trickle of blood leaking onto the floor from under his uniform cap. *Not good* he thought to himself. *Not good at all!*

Outside, skidding to an abrupt stop, Franz stepped out of his Peugeot 508 Fastback with three armed men beside him. Calmly walking over to the immobilized van they opened fire, their automatic FAMAS rifles spitting three-round bursts of 5.56mm gunfire into the vehicle, quickly and efficiently turning the police van into a large slab of Swiss cheese.

Capitaine Kristoff and Monique Lefort, witnessing the John Wick movie sequence unfolding before their eyes, both exited their vehicle, weapons drawn and trained on the gunmen from behind the safety of their open car doors.

"Put your weapons down!" she said, quickly followed by Capitaine Kristoff.

"Put the guns down!"

One gunman, taking a quick look at the two of them,

laughed, pivoted, and let loose a barrage of bullets in their direction, annihilating the car and the pâtisserie window façade behind them. With Capitaine Kristoff calling for immediate backup and Monique Lefort firing off the occasional 9mm round whenever she could, they were well and truly pinned down. Nowhere to run and definitely nowhere else to hide.

Inside the police van, William and the guard were both crouching on the floor, desperately trying to bury themselves into the smallest recesses of the truck under a blanket of bullet-proof vests and protective armor. The FAMAS rounds continued to perforate the van walls, plowing into the truck and riddling the guard's lifeless body on top of them.

The bombardment stopped. William, frantically struggling with his bindings and handcuffs yelled to the first guard who he suspected, like him, had gone momentarily deaf with the drilling and ricocheting of rounds inside their tin can.

"Get me out of these!" he yelled at the guard—but the guard failed to respond.

As William heaved the dead bullet-riddled body off of him and fumbled frantically along the guard's belt buckle for the keys to free himself, the rear door window was smashed through with the stock of a rifle; an army green grenade dropping to the floor through the small shattered opening. He watched it roll menacingly on the ground beside him, his eyes wide in horror at what he was seeing.

"Sinclair says 'Burn in Hell,'" spat Franz, a sadistic smile on his apoplectic rage-ravaged face.

Turning away, Franz sprayed the remainder of his magazine

into Monique Lefort's and Capitaine Kristoff's car, obliterating what was left of its windscreen and bursting the tires that hadn't already exploded in the frenzied attack as they cowered behind the trunk of the car. Speeding up Boulevard Haussmann, the faint whirl of sirens could be heard fast approaching in the distance.

William eyed the green metal F1 grenade rolling ominously on the floor towards him. Still handcuffed, and unable to locate the keys on the dead guard's body he was petrified, absolutely terror-stricken with only seconds remaining to react. With eyes as big as hubcaps and his hands still bound, he figured he had no choice but to pick it up with his mouth! *No time to lose one's head.*

Manically throwing his face onto the explosive device, as if bobbing for apples at a Michael Myers Halloween picnic party, he clenched the grenade between his teeth, heaved himself to his feet, and lunged himself forward towards the opening in the rear window through which the grenade had been dropped. Spitting it out with frenzied determination and panic, he threw himself to the ground and behind the body of a dead guard milliseconds before the device exploded, partially blowing the back doors off their hinges. Dazed and bleeding, he struggled valiantly to keep his senses and wits about him. With blood running from his nose, mouth, and ears he fumbled on the floor for the keys to his handcuffs in order to free himself.

Franz, walking back to his car and ducking from the loud explosion, looked back with satisfaction at the mangled rear doors of the van. Climbing back into the passenger side of his

Peugeot, he disappeared with his men through the gridlocked chaos, unaware that his grenade had not gone off *inside* the van as planned.

As the vehicle sped off, Monique cautiously appeared from behind her decimated car and, gun drawn, slowly and carefully approached the van which was still smoking from the explosion. Capitaine Kristoff, still protected behind the car, stayed on the radio to give a detailed description of the getaway vehicle and its four occupants.

As Monique approached the front of the van she saw that the driver of the vehicle and the guard in the front passenger seat next to him were both dead. Riddled with bullets. Slowly making her way to the rear, her gun drawn and her senses on high alert, she saw her man, on the floor and now free from his bindings, trying to remove the gun from one of the dead guard's holsters.

"Put it down!" she told him.

William looked up and sighed. "You gotta be kidding me."

"I said put it down. Now!"

William, dazed and with ringing still in his ears, smiled. He was beat and had no more fight in him, not even enough to pretend. Offering up the gun he slowly surrendered and placed his hands in the air.

"You win," he told her. "I'm all yours," before collapsing, exhausted, on his back.

A small army of police, gendarmes, and a small GIGN tactical unit were now arriving at the scene amidst a backdrop of investigators who were documenting the area and taking eyewitness reports from everyone at the scene. Reporters and news media cameras flashed from the sidelines. On a gurney, cut, bloodied, and bruised, William Trevor Francis was being tended to by a young medic. Approaching him and removing her handcuffs from her service belt, Monique placed the cold metal bands around his wrist and the gurney railing.

"Take him away. I'll follow," she instructed the medic once he had finished dressing a bloody wound on his patient's face.

The medic nodded as William was lifted into the back of the ambulance. He looked up at her, a glint of mischievousness and admiration in his eyes

"Your bedside manner is appalling. We're going to have to work on that. I'm the victim here."

"If you're the victim then I need a new job," she replied, a hint of sarcasm detectible in her tone. "You're lucky to be alive."

William looked down at his bindings, rattled the metal handcuffs against the gurney railings, and smiled at her.

"Could have fooled me!"

With its sirens blaring, the ambulance nimbly weaved its way down through the small Paris streets, down through Le Marais in the 4th, past the boutiques, galleries, and nightclubs, and over to Châtelet followed by an impressive procession of police cars, sirens, and horns.

William Trevor Francis, relishing the relative peace and tranquility from his bed, rested on his back with his eyes shut, listening to the conversation that was going on between the medic and the police officer beside him. Opening his eyes, he slowly started taking in his surroundings, discreetly working at his fastenings as he formulated his plan.

Feigning a groan, a cough, and a splutter, he writhed in pretend pain. Seeing his face turn blue, the panicked medic rushed to his feet to see what was wrong. As soon as he was within reach, William head-butted him, knocking him to the ground. The accompanying police officer, caught off guard by the sudden and unexpected sequence of events, rushed to restrain him, but William was once again fighting for his life. Fighting for survival.

Kicking the officer squarely in the jaw and managing to lock his freed legs around the police officer's neck, he squeezed as hard as he could until the police officer finally fell, unconscious, to the ground. Still wrestling with his upper torso bindings, William frantically fought to disconnect one of the side rails of the flimsy gurney, kicking at it and pulling it apart with all of his remaining force, the handcuffs around his wrists cutting deep painful gashes into his flesh, his hands dripping with blood.

Finally managing to break one of the bottom corner pipe sections, he slid his hand-cuffed wrist out of the pole and got unsteadily to his feet. The medic, still dazed on the floor and with a broken nose, tried to stop him.

"Don't do it. Don't even think about doing it," he threatened him, pole in hand.

The medic quickly, and wisely backed down.

William looked out of the side ambulance windows. He knew this area. They were crossing the Pont Notre-Dame and the river Seine, headed presumably for the Île de la Cité and the Préfecture de Police with its medical ward on Rue de Lutèce. *Bollocks!* he thought. *Once I'm locked up there I'll never get out.*

Hearing the driver in the front of the cabin calling for immediate backup, he knew it was now or never. He had one shot. One opportunity and he wasn't going to let it go. Grabbing the unconscious officer's gun and pointing it directly at the cowering medic's head beside him he addressed the driver.

"Stop the vehicle or I'll blow his head off."

William knew it was an empty threat, but it had been a bloody long day and he had just about reached his limit, both physically and mentally. Pulling a dirty stunt like this was the last thing he wanted to do, but he was desperate to get the Hell out of that ambulance.

The ambulance screeched to an immediate halt.

Throwing open the rear doors, he saw that he was trapped, a line of squad cars following the ambulance simultaneously slamming on their brakes and forming a semi-circle around him, blocking his escape. He had nowhere to go. Nowhere to run. Even Harry Houdini would have had a hard time escaping from this one. Monique Lefort, Capitaine Kristoff, and what resembled half of the city's police force all exited their vehicles in unison, their guns and assault rifles all trained on the trapped and bloodied lone figure in front of them.

"Freeze! Don't make a move!" said Capitaine Kristoff.

Monique shouted above the slowly growing cacophony of voices.

"William!"

William looked at her and smiled. *Did she actually care about him? Had he detected a little something in her voice? A little 'je ne sais quoi'?*

Jumping out of the ambulance, he made a quick, agile run towards the edge of the bridge and leaped high into the air. Monique and the rest of the officers immediately ran to the bridge's edge, peering down into the dark murky waters below, but the handsome Englishman was nowhere to be seen.

CHAPTER EIGHTEEN

LET'S MEET UP FOR COFFEE

THE NEXT DAY, IN A QUIET BACKSTREET CAFÉ ON THE corner of rue de Grenelle and rue Cler, a brisk 10-minute walk South of the Seine in the 7th arrondissement, William, looking decidedly worse for wear, was propped up at a bar swigging a cold Kronenbourg demi with a side of scotch. He knew this area well—very well—and felt safe in its narrow neighborhood streets and back alleys, only minutes from major roads and the river if he needed to get out in a hurry. Rue Cler had been an old favorite haunt of his, not because it was particularly special in any way but because, as a young kid, this is where he had stayed on his first trip to Paris 'sans adult supervision'. This is where he had grown up. The Hôtel Lévêque—or the Grand Hôtel Lévêque—as it was now called was still there, but it wasn't the overpriced hotel or the narrow street filled with fresh fruits, meats, cheeses, and breads every morning, that kept him coming back. No, it was the memories, the very fond memories of the city that he had formed all those many years ago.

As a fourteen year old boy, William had walked the whole city on foot using the hotel as his basecamp. He had trodden the dog-crap laden streets from the Eiffel Tower to the Sacré-Coeur, from the Sacré-Coeur to Place de la Nation, and from Place de la Nation down to the Tour Montparnasse. Having zigzagged and crisscrossed the entire city center, he had been sure to visit every museum, gallery, church, and monument along the way. It had been a week-long adventure of a lifetime that had changed him forever.

He knocked back his shot and ordered another.

"Rough day?" the barman asked him.

"You could say that. You got a phone around here?"

"In the back."

William took another swig of his beer before slamming the second shot. He had been standing at the deserted bar, minding his own business for the past 20 minutes, but now his mind was made up. Leaving the bar and walking over to the tatty wall-mounted phone by the toilettes he made sure he was alone, dialed, and waited for the switchboard operator to pick up.

"Lieutenant Monique Lefort. Interpol."

"Et vous êtes?" the operator asked.

"I'm the man who's been on the news non-stop for the past week. I made quite a big splash yesterday."

The line went dead for 30 seconds.

"One moment please while I connect you."

He waited, cautiously, before removing his packet of cigarettes and lighting up. As he exhaled two thick jets of smoke through his nostrils his eyes caught the 'No Smoking' sign on the wall next to him. Sighing, he took one last long drag and stubbed it out on the floor with his foot. The line connected again.

"Lieutenant Lefort speaking."

"It's me. I think it's time the two of us had a little heart to heart."

"I'm listening," she said cautiously.

"I'll give you everything I've got on Sinclair. Everything I know. But we're going to do this my way."

Monique fired back. "I told you I'm the one who calls the shots. We'll do this *my* way."

William sighed. "I didn't call to fight with you—and I didn't call to turn myself in. I'll give you what I've got on Sinclair—but that's all. Either you take him down or I do. It's a simple choice."

Monique contemplated the offer. "What do you have in mind?"

"How about we meet up for coffee? Somewhere in the open. I'll let you know when I'm ready. Just make sure you come alone or the deal's off."

With that, he hung up, headed back to the bar, threw a

twenty down on the counter, finished his beer, thanked the bartender, and walked out into the cold and lonely night.

———————

THE PARIS INTERPOL STATION WAS A BUZZ OF ACTIVITY. Monique Lefort hung up her phone with half a dozen officers hanging around her desk, waiting with bated breath, for instructions.

"Did you get his location?" she asked the two men monitoring the phone.

"We can trace it back, but it'll take time," one of the officers said, shaking his head in disappointment.

"How long?" she asked impatiently.

"Five minutes—maybe less," the other officer responded.

"Merde! OK, everyone. Back to work. When this guy makes contact again I want everyone on this. William Trevor Francis does *not* get away. He remains our *top* priority!"

There were nods of agreement from around the room. Everyone present knew what had to be done. Everyone in that room was aware of the consequences if they failed again.

Leaving the group congregated around Monique Lefort's glass-topped office desk, the same young DRI individual who had sold out and reported back to Franz regarding William's initial prison transfer, disappeared into an empty stairwell to make a call.

In the quiet church of Saint-Dominique, located around the corner from the Paris Catacombs in the 14th arrondissement, Franz sat alone on a cold pew, listening to the classical music playlist on his smartphone. His phone rang, interrupting his moment of contemplative solitude.

"Yes?" he said impatiently.

Whispering, the junior officer's voice was barely audible on the other end of the line.

"Contact has been made. A rendezvous is going to be set up. I'll let you know when and where as soon as it's confirmed."

CHAPTER NINETEEN

PLACE DE LA RÉPUBLIQUE

Two days later, William Trevor Francis emerged, in disguise, up the steps from the République Metro station and made his way over to the town square café where Monique Lefort was waiting for him. Looking up admiringly at Marianne, the central female statue in the middle of the square representing France's Liberty, Equality, and Fraternity, he marveled at the bustle of activity around him: skateboarders, souvenir vendors, and musicians all populating the busy and recently renovated pedestrianized 'Place'.

Spotting Monique, seated alone at an outside café table, he headed over to her, pulled up a polished aluminum chair, and sat himself down next to her. It took her a moment to realize who he was.

"Forgive the theatrics, but all of a sudden I've got more followers than the Pope."

Monique looked at him incredulously. "A little dramatic don't you think?"

William laughed. *Just how big was the stick up this girl's arse?* he thought to himself.

"I love the drama, what can I say?"

The waiter, an undercover cop, approached the table just as William was taking out his cigarettes and making himself comfortable.

"Pour monsieur?" he asked.

"Noisette. Double. Merci."

The waiter nodded and left.

William looked over his shoulder at the half-empty restaurant. Something was not right. His guard was up, the red flag in his gut waiving emphatically to be on alert.

"I didn't know whether I could trust you. Whether you'd sell me out or not," he told her.

"What makes you so sure I didn't?"

He looked over his shoulder again and then studied the people on the terraced forecourt.

"To be perfectly honest, I'm not."

"Good. Because I'm not a fool and I won't have you play me for one!"

William genuinely liked this woman. There was something about her. Something special. She was attractive—not in the blonde, big-boobed Barbie-stripper sense that he was usually accustomed to, but in a more refined, sexy, *smart way*. She was also clearly competent at her job and didn't back down from a fight. Truth be told she was proving herself to be a worthy adversary, but the tough talk was beginning to piss him off.

"Is it difficult being this tough all the time?"

"I didn't get to where I am by lying on my back. Now, what have you got for me?"

The waiter returned with the café noisette, setting the milky espresso, sugar cube, and mini biscotti on the table.

William slowly stirred the white cube of sugar into his delicate cup and savored the bittersweet hazelnut-colored coffee.

"Bugger me that's good!" he exclaimed as he pondered what he was going to say next.

"Like I said," he continued, "I believe I have everything you need to tie Gabriel Sinclair and his men to the Allied Laboratories bombing. How he did it and what he stood to gain. I'll connect the dots for you—save you some time."

On the 3rd floor of the Crowne Plaza hotel on the South-Eastern corner of the main square, the barrel of his CZ700 sniper rifle poking through the metal railings of the balcony, Franz picked up his cell phone and called Sinclair for further instructions. With William Trevor Francis squarely in his sights, he could easily have taken 'the shot' twenty times by now, but with the heavy police presence and the INTERPOL association, pulling the trigger would be a decision that only Sinclair could authorize. The implications and the risk for Sinclair were simply too high to leave anything to chance.

"I have him in my sights. He's with a woman. I don't know who she is. Most likely Police from what I can tell," he said, his voice emotionless.

"Take him down and bring her to me. I need to know exactly what she knows," Sinclair responded, matter of factly.

Hanging up, Franz loaded the chamber with his bandaged hand from the car seat fiasco and took aim.

———————————

INSIDE THE CAFÉ, THE UNDERCOVER COPS WERE CLOSELY monitoring Monique Lefort and William Trevor Francis who were now deep in conversation. Capitaine Kristoff was ready to close the net. From his vantage point at a table on the inside with a clear view of his suspect, he spoke, discreetly and authoritatively, into his lapel radio.

"No one moves until I give the order. I want a clean catch."

The undercover agents dotted around inside the café and outside, shuffled with nervous anticipation, readying themselves for the starter's gun.

William was uneasy.

"Listen. I've held up my end of the bargain. Now it's your turn. Are you going to call your men off or do you still think you can take me in?"

Monique looked at him defiantly, the black pupils of her hazel eyes piercing through him..

"I still plan on taking you in. Nothing's changed," she said.

Capitaine Kristoff, sensing that the suspect was becoming increasingly agitated, knew they would have to strike soon if he wanted to apprehend him.

William ripped off his fake Pablo Escobar moustache and

sat back in his chair, oozing the confidence of someone who is fully aware of their surroundings, but indifferent as to how the chess moves would inevitably be played out.

"The waiter to my left is wearing an earpiece. So's the woman at the table by the window on my right. The couple in the unmarked car opposite haven't moved for the past 20 minutes. The café's two-thirds empty but the waiters are still turning customers away when it should be heaving. Now call me paranoid, but this doesn't quite add up does it?"

He studied Monique's face, her soft lip line, her delicately applied eyeliner, her steady breathing, her ample bosom hiding underneath the cream chiffon blouse of her dark blue pantsuit, but she wasn't giving anything away. *She'd make one Hell of a poker player* he thought. *A real pro.*

"Everyone ready to move on my mark," said Capitaine Kristoff, now unhooking the strap of his holster.

"What did you expect? A deal?" she said as she looked into his mischievous brown eyes and studied the course, mottled stubble on his handsomely rugged face. *I bet he considers himself a real ladies' man* she thought to herself. *A real player.*

"No. But a bit of honesty would be nice," he said, interrupting her thoughts.

She laughed, cynically. "Ha! Coming from a thief!"

Capitaine Kristoff gave the order from the back of the room. Speaking into his lapel he finally green-lit the strike and the café erupted.

"Second team, wait for my signal. First team GO!"

As the waiter, a young man in his mid-twenties dropped his tray and trained his gun on William, Monique also reached for hers, total chaos erupting everywhere.

At the Crowne Plaza, Franz took careful aim at William whose head was now neatly quartered in the cross-hairs of his sniper sights. Startled by the sudden and unexpected commotion, he fired a single hurried shot at his target. To his utter dismay and annoyance, it missed its mark and instead hit the young waiter in the head, dropping him to the ground as if unplugged from the Matrix.

Monique instinctively reached for her gun at the sight of the dead officer, as William impulsively threw her to the ground to protect her. All Hell was breaking loose. The quiet Café République had been transformed into a John Woo movie set. Franz furiously fired again and again in quick succession, but the upheaval in the café was throwing him off, his bullets missing their mark and ricocheting off the walls, tables, and chairs, tearing the café's insides to tatters.

Outside the café the two undercover police officers, parked in their unmarked car, jumped out of their vehicle, guns drawn, ready to return fire—if only they knew where the shots were coming from. People across the square and in the streets screamed hysterically as they ran and ducked for cover.

"Where is that gunfire coming from?" screamed Capitaine Kristoff from behind an upturned table. "What the Hell is going on?"

His senior officer responded immediately from behind the

bar "No idea Capitaine. I think they're coming from across the square."

"Where's the suspect? Do you have him?"

The senior officer carefully stole a quick glance at the outside table, but William and Monique had both fled the scene.

"Merde!" he exclaimed. "No Capitaine. Negative."

WILLIAM AND MONIQUE WERE HALFWAY ACROSS THE main square, running frantically between pedestrians, painters, and photographers before Franz spotted them; William dragging Monique by the arm, pushing people out of the way as he guided them both to safety. Franz fired two successive shots at his moving target, the first round hitting the ground with a puff of dust, the second finding a suitable victim. Maniacally he grabbed his walkie-talkie and screamed into it.

"Targets are heading across the main square towards the North-West corner. Get the woman. The Englishman is mine. I repeat, take the woman but do not stop the Englishman. He's mine!"

Monique moaned as she collapsed onto her knees in the middle of the square. "William!" she yelled.

He slowed down and stopped pulling. She was bleeding. She had been hit. Looking around desperately for cover he scooped her up in his arms and carried her into a nearby shop entrance where they were both protected from further possible gunfire.

"Let me have a look at that," he said calmly.

Ripping her blouse open he examined the bullet wound. Monique, in shock, trembling and on the verge of tears was struggling to keep it together.

"Is it bad?" she asked.

"No. You'll be fine. It's gone straight through" he said while tearing a sleeve from her shoulder and wrapping it around the open wound to stop the bleeding.

He looked into her eyes, reassuringly. "I'll buy you a new one!"

They both looked at each other and, for a split second, formed a connection that neither of them could have anticipated. In the background, fast approaching on foot, William saw five other officers closing in on him fast. He had no choice but to leave her behind if he had any chance of escaping. He hesitated for a split second and considered kissing her on the lips, possibly on the cheek, maybe even on the forehead, but decided against all three. Instead, he looked her straight in her big dark doe-eyes and gave her his word.

"I'll fix this Monique, I promise!" And with that, he was gone.

———————

WILLIAM TREVOR FRANCIS WAS NOW BEING CHASED ON foot across Place de la République by the police from the café as an unmarked van screeched to a halt in front of Monique. Capitaine Kristoff, unable to reach the vehicle in time, witnessed her being thrown through the sliding doors of the van. Panting and out of breath, he watched with horror as it sped off around the corner and down Boulevard de Magenta.

"Merde!" he yelled at the top of his voice, unable to control his anger. "Get a description of that van on the radio. Now!" he shouted at the fellow officer who had just run the 100m in Usain Bolt time in order to catch up with him. Capitaine Kristoff was torn. His primary suspect was now fleeing on foot across the main square, but his partner had just been kidnapped. His very own Sophie's choice.

"After him!" he screamed at the remaining officers, now all circling around him, before reporting back to the station on his hand-held radio.

William continued charging on foot through the multitude of people in his way, hurtling over benches and plowing into vendors and their stalls as the ensuing police officers slowly but surely caught up with him. Franz, now back in his black Jaguar and watching everything from across the square in a side street, started his engine and drove off, hanging back just enough to watch the chase play out.

William, still on the run with his legs and lungs on fire, desperately out of breath and with a killer stitch in his side mustered all of his remaining strength and courage as he careered on foot across the main pedestrian bridge, along Quai de Valmy, and over the Canal Saint-Martin. Running out in front of a small Lego-looking Smart car, idling along in slow afternoon traffic, he forced it to an abrupt stop.

"Out!" he told the driver.

The driver, an older man in his sixties, scared but belligerent, protested as he was forcibly dragged from his car.

"Tu peux pas faire ça. Arrête. C'est ma voiture!" he protested, in vain.

"Désolé, mate."

The driver tried valiantly to fight, but William kept him at arm's length.

"Don't!" he said, calmly, but convincingly.

The old man backed down and watched helplessly as his carjacker jumped into the driver's seat, rammed the gears into first, and launched the tin can on wheels up onto the pavement, along the canal bank, and back onto the main road, past the hospital on his left and towards the Parc des Buttes-Chaumont.

CHAPTER TWENTY

FANCY A CUPPA?

POLICE CARS, SIRENS BLARING WERE NOW HOT ON William's heels as he floored his 0.9L, 3-cylinder jam-jar along Avenue Claude Vellefaux headed due North. Expertly slipping the clutch through the tight 5-speed manual gearbox, he maneuvered the car back off the main Avenue and down through the side streets of the 19th arrondissement. As he continued to race through the busy streets, weaving his way through traffic and pedestrians, he hit a standstill and made the split-second decision to bump the Smart car back up onto the curb, crashing, once again, through the vendor stalls and shop front displays in his path.

Startled by a stray dog that had just run out in front of him he swerved instinctively, causing his box-car to take a nose-dive into the front of the Buttes Chaumont underground metro entrance. Crashing down the concrete steps and wedging itself in the narrow, intricately designed wrought iron entrance, the deceptively powerful airbag deployed, punching him in the face like Manny Pacquiao.

Fighting his way around the now deflated airbag and unable to open his car door, he pummeled desperately at the broken windscreen with his hand, knocking the glass clean out of its frame. He had to get out of there. He was a sitting duck. Scrambling on all fours through the empty cavity he slid over the front of the car's short stubby hood and raced down the subway entrance towards the ticket barriers leaving his car stuck in the entrance behind him like a cork in a bottle of wine. With a lone police officer descending the dark stairwell above him, the chase was on once again!

Jumping the stairs two at a time and weaving his way through the many passengers, he descended into the belly of the metro station, hurdled the ticket barrier, and threw himself down the escalator. He felt like he was dying. On his last legs. Severely out of breath, his lungs burning white-hot, sweat cascading down his face, he knew he needed a different career. He really should give up smoking. *It's killing me, quite literally* he thought to himself. With his energy and pace quickly diminishing, the gap between him and the police officer chasing him was narrowing. Forty meters, thirty meters.

Running the long length of the white-tiled tunnel, the solitary policeman on foot now only twenty meters behind him, he turned the corner onto the empty platform entrance and jumped into an open carriage just as the heavy hydraulic doors were shutting. The deflated officer, only mere seconds behind him, rounded the corner to see his target rolling out of the metro station.

"Incroyable!" he yelled in total frustration. "Incroyable!"

William, with his lungs on fire, his legs aching, sweat pouring off of him, white as a ghost, hardly able to catch his breath, collapsed onto an empty seat, unable to fathom, genuinely unable to comprehend, just how lucky his escape had been. Fellow passengers on the train eyed him wearily, keeping their distance, mindful of this seemingly mad man. Slowly coming to his senses he composed himself, checked the underground map above the door, exited at the first stop, doubled back on another train, and eventually, forever mindful of the CCTV cameras at each tunnel entrance and exit, emerged above ground, hidden in a crowd of commuters, into the early evening hours. It had been a long day.

Visibly worn out and exhausted, he trudged the quiet, lonely path, and contemplated the day's dismal events. The flickering on of street lamps was now emitting a subdued soft glow in the peaceful chill of the night air. In the distance, a few remaining shop owners flipped their store signs from 'ouvert' to 'fermé'. His ears pricked at the sound of laughter coming from the outdoor patio seating of a nearby café. Two lovers, smoking cigarettes, drinking rosé, and sharing kisses under the warmth of a shared blanket caught his attention. *Oh, to be young and in love, in Paris,* he mused, envious of the carefree, fun-loving, and deeply passionate couple that were oblivious to the world around them. Lifting the collar to his jacket in an attempt to shield his face from the cold air, he continued his long and lonely walk in the shadows of the night, humming Édith Piaf's iconic La Vie En Rose under his breath.

———————

Two days later, William had left the mayhem and madness of Paris and had discreetly made his way back across the border to Berlin. Paris—and France in general—was simply too hot for him right now. He needed to stay low, he needed to stay hidden and he needed to come up with a better long-term plan. Outside the Club Exotica, with his jacket collar pulled high above his cheekbones, he removed his battered pack of smokes and lit up, the flame from his lighter briefly illuminating the rough and worn features of his face. The man had definitely seen better days!

From the shadows he watched as the coat-clad strippers from the club started spilling out of the side entrance, some in a good mood, chatting loudly after a decent night's work; others not so fortunate. It was just past 2 am. Watching them pass him by, he waited for Cindy who, unaccompanied, was now walking up the empty street alone. He waited, watched, and then tailed her from a distance observing all the while that she—and he—were not, in turn, being followed by the authorities. There was a thin line between paranoia and caution and he was treading it finely.

Keeping his distance, he followed Cindy to her two bed-room apartment and watched from the shadows as she let herself in. Observing her flick the main hall light, he continued to watch carefully, her silhouette visible through the thin floral drapes, as she made her way from the living room to the bedroom and then to the kitchen. Satisfied that she was alone and that neither he, nor she, had been tailed from the club, he crossed the deserted road and entered the quiet apartment complex.

The lobby corridor was dark, but not unpleasant, the building itself a modern and functional complex that must have been erected during the late eighties or early nineties. When he had first started looking for an apartment for her and Max he had mainly taken into account the quiet single-family orientated neighborhood and its proximity to the local school and supermarket. The neighborhood hadn't changed much over the years and he was pleased to notice that the property itself, as well as the surrounding area, had been adequately maintained. It had been a good choice back then and was still a good choice now. He knocked on the door and waited.

"Wer ist da?" she asked from behind the closed door.

"It's Will."

Cindy peered through her spy hole and cautiously opened the door keeping the chain firmly in place.

"What are you doing here? Do you know what time it is?"

"Yeah. I'm sorry. I need your help."

Satisfied that he was alone, and concerned for his well-being, she unhooked the security chain and let him in.

"My God. What's happened to you?"

"Long story."

"You know the police are after you?"

"Err—yeah," he said, rather sarcastically.

"Was that you in Paris at the shootout? On TV?"

"Yeah."

"Jesus. You'd better come in."

He entered and, noticing a small collection of her and Max's shoes by the doorway, removed his own shoes before sitting down on the plush lilac-colored sofa in her living room, his body immediately melting into the oversized cushions like cold butter on hot toast.

"What are you doing in Berlin?" she asked inquisitively.

"I'm sorry, but I had nowhere else to go. I'll be gone as soon as possible. I promise."

Cindy paused. This man had done so much for her without ever asking for anything in return. A real Robin Hood. The least she could do was offer him her sofa for the night.

"Max asleep?" he asked.

"No. He stays at my mother's over the weekend. I'll pick him up on Monday."

"How's he doing? Enjoying school?"

"Yeah. You know. Kids can be mean. But he's doing better than he was at the last one."

"You want me to bust a few heads? Teach those ten-year-old's a lesson for him?"

"Nah. I think I'll let him sort it out. The last thing he needs is a wanted criminal as a bodyguard," she laughed. "You want a drink while I clean those cuts up? Then you can tell me everything from the beginning."

William sighed contentedly. For now, mercifully, he was safe.

"That would be great."

Cindy got up, crossed to her kitchen, and removed a half-empty bottle of Belvedere Vodka from her freezer. She poured a single glass for him and reentered her living room only to find him fast asleep on her sofa.

"Typical," she sighed under her breath, before setting the drink down on the table next to him and retrieving her first aid kit from the bathroom.

The next day, lying comfortably on the sofa with a blanket draped over him, William slowly opened his eyes and took in his surroundings. The apartment was clean and quiet, save the sound of soft music coming from the bathroom. Sitting upright, he placed his feet on the ground and held his head in his hands trying to remember all the steps that had brought him here. Mistaking the vodka for water, he grabbed the glass on the table next to him and took a long thirsty gulp. Instinctively, he dry heaved and shuddered.

"Bollocks!" he sputtered, repulsed at the taste of neat vodka first thing in the morning.

Slowly, and in obvious pain, he got to his feet, crossed to the kitchen, and put the kettle on for a cup of tea. Checking his face in the mirror by the kitchen entrance, he took stock of his many cuts and scrapes that had been both cleaned and dressed. *What a mess!*

The bathroom door opened and Cindy, wrapped in a luxuriously oversized pink fleece bathrobe, a towel secured around her head emerged through a bellow of hot steam. She could easily have been in an '80's Whitesnake video. She looked beautiful, the real beauty that requires no makeup, no effort.

"Well finally. I thought you'd never wake up," she said, acknowledging his presence in the kitchen.

"How long was I asleep for?"

"A good eleven hours. You must have needed it."

"Yeah. I think I did," he responded. "Listen, I'm sorry for coming here last night. For just turning up like that."

"Don't worry about it. But I would like some answers before I head out for work."

"Of course. Fancy a cuppa first? I've just put the kettle on."

"Sure, tea and coffee are in the cupboard by the fridge. I'll take a tea."

Opening the cupboard he saw a mixed assortment of herbal teas and instinctively pulled a face, a mixture of horror and disgust. Not a 'British Blend' in sight. Looked like he'd be having instant coffee instead.

"I'm surprised you didn't call the police last night," he said, genuinely impressed.

"I thought about it."

He handed her a steeping cup of chamomile tea and took a sip of his coffee, the treacle-like liquid instantly removing the top layer of enamel from his teeth. It was disgusting.

"So what are you involved in? The police came to the club and questioned us all about Vinny's death."

"That wasn't me Cindy. I swear."

"I know it wasn't. You think I'd have let you in if I thought it was?"

"No. You're smarter than that."

She nodded her head in agreement. "So what's going on?"

Placing his cup of mud on the table beside him, he began to recount and explain the sequence of events as best he could, telling her as much as he deemed was safe.

"I always knew you were trouble," she groaned when he had finished.

He looked at her and grinned, inquisitively.

"So you're not going to turn me in?"

"If I was going to do that I'd have done it already. Now, how are those cuts doing?"

"Sore. But I've had worse."

"Let me take another look at them," she said attentively while removing the heavy cotton towel from her head.

Standing in front of him she slowly and delicately started inspecting the band-aids on his temple, his cheek, and his knuckles. The captivating smell of her lavender and bergamot shampoo on her wet tousled hair, the clean hint of spearmint on her breath, the soapy fragrance of her smooth skin was driving him crazy with desire. He was enthralled. Captivated. Looking deep into her eyes, and she into his, they kissed passionately, his hands softly caressing her shoulders and the back of her neck before making their way down the inside of her open robe. Gently removing his wandering hands, she slowly and seductively unfastened her belt, allowing her bathrobe to fall, invitingly, to the ground.

CHAPTER TWENTY ONE

I WANT YOU

WILLIAM TREVOR FRANCIS STOOD AT THE OPEN WINDOW, futilely trying to blow the smoke from his cigarette into the wind. He flicked the butt into the street below, fanned the air for good measure, and closed the window. *Who was he kidding? Of course she'd smell it.*

Switching on the small Samsung television set in the corner of the living room, he searched for a news station to get himself caught up but amid the German dubbed Colombo, a few chintzy shopping channels, a rather good soft-porn channel, and an in-depth analysis of the current housing market, there wasn't anything that grabbed his attention. Well—maybe the soft porn. Disappointed by the lack of news coverage, he got up and went back into the kitchen to fix himself a bite to eat, flicking on a small AM/FM digital radio as he crossed to the refrigerator. Making himself a simple cheese and ham sandwich, he poured himself a glass of Spezi and sat down at the small kitchen table in the middle of the room as the hourly news headlines sounded through the radio speakers.

He took a hearty bite of his sandwich and listened intently

as the female reporter started her coverage of the news head-lines and top stories so far.

"And now more on the Paris story that has gripped the headlines. Senior officials dealing with the case have just confirmed that one of their lead officers connected with the inquiry was kidnapped at the site of the Paris town square shooting on Thursday."

"Shit!" he exclaimed, a mouthful of sandwich falling from his open mouth.

"Details are still emerging as to the specifics surrounding the event, but Capitaine Kristoff with INTERPOL's National Central Bureau in Paris has confirmed that a top ranking female agent was abducted at the scene of the shooting and that William Trevor Francis, their primary suspect, remains at large."

"Bloody Hell!" he exclaimed again, more half-chewed sandwich falling from his mouth.

"For more details on this case we go now to Virginie Durand, reporting live in Paris from the Place de la République where the shooting and abduction took place."

William threw his sandwich down on the plate and slammed his fist on the table next to it.

"Oh, for crying out loud!"

When Cindy returned home in the early hours of the morning after her shift at the club, William was dressed and waiting for her under the soft glow of a lampstand in her living room. The television was on but the sound had been muted.

Entering the room she immediately sensed that there was a problem.

"What's wrong?" she asked, removing her coat and hanging it up on a rack in the hallway.

"I have to go, Cindy."

"What, now? It's almost three in the morning."

"I wanted to say goodbye and to thank you in person."

"What's wrong?"

"Something's happened. Something I have to deal with."

Cindy, resilient as she was, now had tears in her eyes. She tried her best to fight them back.

"And what about me?" she asked. "What am I supposed to do?"

"Cindy, I'll make it up to you. I promise. I'll pay you back."

Unable to hold back her emotions she began to tear up. Walking over to him she threw herself into his arms.

"I don't want your money. I want *you*."

Gently pushing her back he tried to be as sincere and straight with her as he could.

"I can't my luv. Not now. There's a ton of shit happening all around me and people are getting hurt. It wouldn't be fair on you."

She sobbed into his chest as he caressed her hair and kissed the top of her head.

"I just wanted to say thank you before I left."

Reaching for his jacket that was draped over the couch she asked one last question.

"Will I see you again?"

William paused and smiled.

"I hope so."

Kissing her one last, long time on the lips, he exited the room and closed the front door behind him, leaving Cindy all alone.

CHAPTER TWENTY TWO

HOME SWEET HOME

WILLIAM TREVOR FRANCIS LANDED AT GATWICK AIRPORT the next day in disguise under another alias. Under normal circumstances he would have avoided the major airports like the plague, preferring instead to enter the UK via ferry from either France, Belgium, or Ireland, but under the circumstances and with time fighting against him, he had decided to take the necessary risk and chance it. So far so good.

Being back in England always gave him mixed emotions. He loved the city passionately, having lived and been educated there since he was nine, but being back home always filled him with a melancholy feeling of disappointment and regret. Raised in the small, suburban village of Cheam, Surrey—notable for its once-famed Nonsuch Palace, built under Henry VIII—he had attended Epsom College during his teenage years, a period that had profoundly changed his life and set him on a new path forever.

The College, founded in 1853 had many noteworthy accolades to its rich history—including having Queen Elizabeth II as its patron—but it had been the rugby, beer, and girls that had excited him the most—and which had later proven to be his downfall. Having excelled at the former three with flying colors, his academic grades and chances of success with a top University had gone to shit, dive-bombing into the ground in a ball of fire.

This, combined with a rather unfortunate and acrimonious divorce on his home front had, in turn, led him to be a rather aggressive, confrontational, and 'misunderstood teenager'. Some would even say 'a dick'. Flunking his exams quite horrifically—he wasn't a *bad* student, he was just a *lazy* student— he had decided in a bull-headed shit-or-bust kind of way to volunteer for French National Service using his mother's nationality and his French country of birth to 'reinvent himself'.

The cause-and-effect of his early career choices had been set in motion. University black-tie clubs and societies that he could have enjoyed had given way to grueling forced marches, blood-soaked socks, and more tactical training than he could possibly have imagined. But what would his life have been like if he had stayed on the narrow, predictable path? How would his life have panned out if he had knuckled down, done the work, and stayed in the fold? It was a question that always clouded his thoughts whenever he set foot back in Blighty.

Stepping outside of the airport, he pulled the collar of his jacket up around his ears, retrieved his pack of smokes, and lit up, exhaling with a heavy sigh, the blue smoke slowly dissipating into the brisk evening air. *You could take the boy outta London, but you'd never take London outta the boy!*

Hailing a black cab, he contemplated his life and his life choices as he watched the night suburban lights wash past him. Descending the A217 through Banstead, he instructed the cabbie to pull over and to drop him off outside the Sutton train station. Whenever he was in town and feeling pensive he always enjoyed a quick pint in the Old Bank pub which sat side by side with the station's entrance. Growing up, his father and he had enjoyed many lively conversations and heated debates at the bar, and now he was allowing himself the opportunity to reminisce about 'the good times' over a pint of Fuller's Pride. To his enormous delight, the pub and its boisterous patrons hadn't changed a bit in all those years. Dad may have gone, but his memory lived on.

Stepping back outside after his quick pit stop, he hailed a second black taxi from the adjacent taxi rank, hopped in, and told the driver to head over to Cheam Village, a short 10-minute drive away. Pulling into the enclosed parking lot of The Harrow pub on the corner of the village's main crossroads, he slipped the driver a decent tip and then watched and waited as he reversed out and rejoined the flow of traffic.

After a few minutes of careful surveillance, satisfied that he hadn't been followed, he walked to the rear of the car park, jumped the 7-foot red brick wall, and proceeded along the narrow back hedgerow to the main Highstreet, exiting 8 shops down at what had once been the Showtime VHS movie rental shop. Crossing the street, he made his way to the block of apartments overlooking Anne Boleyn's Walk and Kings Way. The night was still, the occasional burst of raucous laughter coming from the Prezzo and The Star of India restaurants over the road.

Punching the outside keypad code, he checked once more that he was alone and then entered the building, jogging up the steps to his third-floor flat. His small 'pied-à-terre' was immaculate. Hidden in the quiet, sleepy suburb that he knew like the back of his hand, he had everything he needed within arm's reach, whatever his circumstances. It was his safe haven. His retreat. His tiny little oasis of comfort and tranquility. Shutting and bolting the heavy door behind him, he disabled the security alarm, kicked over the pile of envelopes, mailers and flyers on the floor in front of him, and removed his well-worn and trusty black leather coat, herringbone cap, and grey checkered Burberry cashmere scarf.

Tired and disheveled, he walked over to his liquor trolley, removed a large bottle of Laphroaig Cask-Strength, poured himself a heavy three fingers, and switched on his BBC Sounds app. *Time for a little Jeremy Vine* he thought. Always a favorite of his. Always enjoyable, and like him, also an Old Epsomian. Taking a long pull at his dark drink, embracing the burn of the neat whisky as it hit the bottom of his empty stomach he looked out through his large bay windows, across the park, and over the majestic skyline of London—Canary Wharf and Battersea Power Station both bright beacons in the dark blanket of night.

Allowing his head to flop back against the plump cushion

of the sofa he closed his eyes, cleared his mind, and focused his attention on the news topic of the hour. He sighed in dismay at the sorry state of world affairs, poured himself another large scotch, and enjoyed the momentary dulling of his senses as the warm whisky worked its magic. At the end of the thoroughly depressing news coverage, the radio host played R.E.M's 'It's The End Of The World'. *Brilliant,* he thought to himself as he took another long, slow sip of his drink, closed his eyes, and hummed along to the tune. *Bloody brilliant!*

Snapping himself back to reality, he walked over to the South-facing wall, measured out four palm widths to the right of an original Turner watercolor of Windsor Castle, measured three down, and punched his fist through the wallpaper-covered drywall. Carefully enlarging the hole, chunk by broken chunk, he removed the black canvas bag from within the cavity and threw it on the floor next to his feet. On the other side of the room, he ran his foot along the wooden eggshell lacquered skirting board behind the dark espresso brown leather sofa, and with an almighty kick, loosened one of the wooden panels.

Getting on his hands and knees, he ripped the skirting board away from the wall and retrieved a second smaller bundle from its deep depths. Taking both bags to the bedroom he carefully emptied the money—in bundles of various currencies—two passports, his old military PAMAS-G1 handgun, four clips, five boxes of 9mm ammo, and his trusty combat knife onto the bed in front of him.

Working the mechanics of the handgun and taking stock of his inventory, he neatly placed all of the contents back into one bag and carried it into the living room, placing it on the floor in front of the window. Pouring himself one last neat whiskey, he sat down and gazed, deep in thought, at the view in front of him and pondered the inevitable, blood-soaked path that lay ahead.

CHAPTER TWENTY THREE
ENOUGH OF THIS

Outside of Gabriel Sinclair's main Swiss residence in Zürich, four armed guards, each toting the new super-sexy Uzi Pro, and each illuminated under the soft glare of the main building lights, could be seen on the top perimeter wall. One armed man for each corner.

William Trevor Francis, dressed in black boots, black pants, a midnight blue commando sweater, and sporting his ATN night vision goggles, slowly grappled his way up and over the outer residence wall. Observing another two armed guards pacing up and down along the gravel path between the main building and the rim of the lawn hedgerow, he crouched, waited, and then proceeded cautiously along the inner rim of the wall, using the foliage from the lush vegetation around him as cover from the clear night sky above. Choosing his moment carefully, he made a long-distance dash across the vast expanse of lawn towards the main residence.

Rolling behind a low-cut and immaculately manicured border hedge, he crawled on his stomach towards the main power box attached to the building that he had been looking for while studying the building and its possible points of access.

Picking the lock, he studied the multitude of colored wires hidden behind the breaker panel, grabbed his wire cutters, and holding his breath, snipped the first two wires. No alarm. That was always a good sign! Satisfied, he continued to cut and rewire a further six wires in sequence—closing the power box and burying himself into the base of a nearby boxwood bush just in time.

William froze with his face in the dirt and held his breath, as a lone guard rounded the corner, his polished toe caps only inches away from William's face. Taking note of the power box, but seeing nothing out of the ordinary, the guard continued with his security rounds, leaving William to sigh heavily and brush himself down.

Expertly tossing his grappling hook above him he nimbly climbed the rope, quickly and efficiently reaching the lower rooftop ledge.

Wary of the cameras and security guards, he crossed the rooftop's ridge, using the black shadows cast by the ventilation units and ductwork to his advantage, and descended into the belly of the building's courtyard below. Attaching a wire rope from his harness to a secure holding, he gently eased himself down, inch by inch, meter by meter until he was able to run the wall and fix another stabilizing rope to the far side, parallel with an outer lobby window. He stopped, suspended in mid-air between the two wires. *Tom Cruise, eat your heart out!*

Fifteen meters below him, in the gently lit courtyard, an armed security guard stopped and spoke into his walkie-talkie.

"Patrol four. Clear. Over."

William, hanging like a pheasant in the butcher's shop window, waited for the guard to continue before removing his knife from its scabbard. Ramming it into the side of the window lock he hammered it home with the pummel of his fist and, holding his breath, slowly pried it open. No alarm. He'd cut the right wires. He exhaled a sigh of relief through his clenched pearly whites.

Unhooking himself from his fastenings, he carefully stepped through the small open window and into Gabriel Sinclair's home—the lion's den—the dark hallway landing made even more so by the deep mahogany wood paneling on the walls. The moonlight cast from outside was just enough to guide him. PAMAS at the ready, he tiptoed along the landing and up the stairs to a second longer hallway, undistinguishable noises coming from somewhere further down.

Peering through the open doors lining the hallway he advanced, gun at the ready, to a quiet office; a small desk lamp gently illuminating the lone figure within. He entered, the muzzle of his pistol pointed squarely at his target.

From behind the door, the tip of a Beretta gently kissed his right temple. *Bollocks! Rookie move!* he thought, furious with himself. *Always check behind the bloody door!*

"At last, you bastard, you're mine," said Franz, slowly stepping out from his dark recess and removing the gun from William's hand.

"Hands on your head."

Doing as instructed, William slowly raised his hands above his head as he watched the man behind the desk slowly raise himself out of his chair.

"You arrogant fool," said Sinclair, venom, and contempt in his voice. "You must have known I'd be waiting for you. What did you think you'd accomplish by coming here?"

"Well, I was rather hoping to kill you," responded William without missing a beat.

Sinclair, vaguely amused by the flippant retort, reached across his desk and removed a Montecristo Herederos from a heavily lacquered humidor.

"I admire your optimism," he said, carefully snipping and lighting the 47-ring gauge Cuban cigar with his Dupont double-torch cigar lighter.

He exhaled a puff of rich blue smoke and took another deliberate draw as he reflected on the run-up to this specific late-night rendezvous.

"You were supposed to die in that explosion. A notorious thief found dead at the scene of the crime. Years of research down the drain and a shorted stock against Allied Laboratories leading to the most profitable quarter my company has seen in years. But you couldn't 'just die' could you?"

"Not my style."

"Impressive," Sinclair mused. "Annoying, but impressive."

"Why me?" William asked.

Sinclair grinned. "You're expendable. You have the highest reputation amongst the lowest people—and I'm sure there are plenty of people you've stolen from over the years who would be happy to see you dead."

"Can't argue with that," he agreed. "Where's Monique?"

"For now, exactly where I want her. Her fate's no concern of yours."

Sinclair took another long, deliberate draw on his cigar. "You should be more worried about your own. You've caused Franz here a lot of headaches."

"The pleasure's all mine."

Sinclair nodded to Franz who was still holding his gun to the back of William's head.

"Take him to the lake. And for God's sake finish him off this time."

William knew the odds were against him, but he wasn't going down without a fight. That simply wasn't in his nature. Failure, and defeat, simply weren't part of his DNA. Sure he could lose. We could all lose. But if he was going down it would be going down fighting to the last breath, to the last drop of blood. That's who he was, that's who he'd always been: a fighter.

As Franz pushed the barrel of the gun into his temple, William pivoted, and with his left arm swiped the gun away from him, knocking it to the floor. In one fluid motion, he launched his clenched fist at Franz's exposed esophagus, but missed the mark completely. Dismayed, but wasting no time, he threw himself on top of Franz, the two men crashing into the study wall and wall-mounted bookcase—fixtures and ornaments falling to the ground and smashing all around them. Franz, it appeared, wasn't going down without a fight either and was gaining the upper hand.

Unleashing a relentless and ruthless barrage of blows onto William's back, William collapsed to his knees—only to be served a hefty dose of kneecap to the face. Falling backwards onto the floor, Franz seized the opportunity to kick him repeatedly in the rib cage and upper torso. Spitting bile and blood, William began cursing the day he was born.

As Franz's right foot came in to deliver another Beckham-style blow to his head, William managed to catch it just in the nick of time before it knocked him for six. Twisting the ankle and bringing Franz to the ground, he grabbed Franz's left arm and then used his right hand to force his shoulder socket against itself, snapping it like a chicken wing. Franz screamed in agony as William wrestled his head into a headlock between his legs and then squeezed with all his remaining might.

Franz, turning purple in the process, fumbled frantically on the ground for the fallen Beretta, grabbed it, and fired—but his attempt was futile—the slug missing William's head and instead burying itself into the wooden wall paneling behind him.

Before he could let off a second round, William grabbed the combat knife from his waistband and, using all of his strength, buried the seven-inch blade between Franz's ribs, twisting the blade and hammering the hilt home for good measure. Exhausted, he waited and watched as the fight, and then the life, slowly drained out of the gargling and spluttering body. It was over. He'd won. He'd survived.

Retrieving the pistol, William slowly got to his feet, steadied himself, and faced Sinclair who was still standing behind his desk, frozen to the spot, unable to fathom what had just happened. Hearing the sound of fast-approaching running in the distance, William took two steps back against the wall, assuming the same hidden position as Franz had done behind the door, and held his gun at arm's length, head height.

A lone guard, responding to the gunshots he had heard, came running down the hallway towards the office. With his gun drawn and at the ready he rushed into the office only to be greeted by a single, decisive shot to the back of the head. He dropped to the ground, a Jackson Pollock arc of blood and brains splashing the paneled walls.

William stepped forward and, with his gun now leveled at Sinclair, approached the desk between them.

"Enough of this," he said matter of factly, "Fuck you and everything you stand for."

The single shot resonated throughout the building as the armed guards below readied themselves for Armageddon.

CHAPTER TWENTY FOUR

YOU READY FOR THIS?

CUT, BEATEN, AND BLOODIED, WILLIAM TREVOR FRANCIS was ready for the showdown of his life as he walked, gun at the ready, out of the office and down the hallway. As a second guard came running up the stairs towards him, he fired a single shot with pinpoint accuracy, and the guard dropped to the ground, eliminated from the game of life.

As William descended the wooden central staircase a third guard rounded the corner firing a heavy stream of bullets from his Uzi, the lead slugs ripping apart the banister, the wall paintings, and artwork but all missing their mark. With a deadly efficient double-tap, it was game over for him too.

At the bottom of the staircase, he crossed the elaborately parqueted floor and made his way over to what appeared to be the empty guard's surveillance room; its bank of black and white security monitors flickering on the wall, a rack of car keys hanging in a grey metallic cabinet beneath it.

Scanning the screens, he quickly identified the basement room that Monique Lefort was being held captive in, seconds before the monitor screens shattered into a thousand shards from gunfire coming from his right. The room and its contents were being ripped to shreds. Instinctively dropping to the ground he belly crawled his way through the broken glass to the sidewall, out of the direct line of fire, as the room around him continued to get blown to smithereens.

Breathing hard and straining all of his senses, he peered through a freshly made bullet hole in the wall, stuck the snub nose of his pistol up against it, and fired. The fourth guard, who had been emptying his submachine gun into the security guard's room like Scarface, dropped to the ground in screams of pain clutching what remained of his mangled manhood. In a split second, William was on his feet and sprinting around the corner. With another professional double-tap, the high-pitched screaming stopped.

Bending down, he ripped the semi-automatic from the guard's hands. *Say hello to my little friend* he grinned to himself. Admittedly, it wasn't the AR15 with grenade launcher that Tony Montana had used, but he's always wanted an Uzi, and this time he was bloody well going to have one!

Weapon in hand, William made his way down to the dimly lit basement uninterrupted, an eerie silence now weighing heavily over the property. Locating Monique's room was easy, as it was the only room with light escaping from around the door frame. Plus it was the only one bolted shut. She screamed as he slid the metal bolt and opened the door—not realizing who it was.

"Want to get out of here?" he said, a cheeky grin on his blood-splattered face.

"Yes!"

The two of them reached the top of the basement stairs and paused, waiting for an ambush, before crossing the main floor with the dead guard spread-eagled unceremoniously in the middle. Crossing to the front door, he quietly pried it open and stole a quick glance outside. It was deadly quiet everywhere. Too quiet for his liking. Checking his options once more, he spotted a black Range Rover parked on the gravel courtyard. It was farther away than he would have liked.

"Shit!"

"Do you have a plan?" she asked him.

William turned to her. "Not really."

"Merde!" she added in agreement.

William studied the car in front of him, grinning as an idea sprang to mind.

"Bear with me," he said, as he ran back towards the security guard's room and grabbed all of the key fobs from the cabinet.

"You ready for this?" he asked, once back by Monique Lefort's side.

"No."

"Good. Neither am I!"

"Merde," she muttered again with a heavy sigh.

Running and pressing the unlock button of each key fob in turn, tossing the wrong ones to the ground along the way, the lights to the Range Rover lit up the courtyard on the fourth attempt, just as the complex sprang back to life. With alarm bells ringing, flood lamps on full beam, and a blistering barrage of gunfire coming towards them, William pushed Monique into the passenger seat and out of harm's way as a storm of bullets ripped through the Carpathian Grey bodywork of her open car door.

Punching the ignition button and slamming the accelerator, pedal to the metal, the Range Rover spat mud, gravel, and grass into the air in equal measure as the two of them charged towards the closed gates.

"Head down!" he shouted at her, more gunfire shattering his windscreen and drilling into the car as he punched his way through the main wrought iron gates and out onto the deserted road ahead.

Screeching down the main road and away from the house, he checked the rearview mirror. No one was following.

"You OK?" he asked as Monique sat back upright, shaking shards of broken glass from her hair.

"Yes. A lot better now."

"Glad to hear it." A smile now cracking his stern face as the two of them looked into each other's eyes.

A sharp pain in his left side caused him to wince. Putting his hand inside his left breast pocket he checked his fingertips for blood. They were red.

"Bugger."

"You need a doctor," she told him concernedly.

"I'll be fine. Let's get you sorted out first."

Reaching inside his pockets again he retrieved his crushed packet of smokes. He lit one up, savoring the moment, then coughed heavily as the thick smoke filled his bruised and battered lungs.

"Those things'll kill you. You really should give them up."

William looked at Monique in disbelief, the cigarette hanging from his split and swollen lips.

"Seriously?" he said, his battered and bloodied face looking more Pablo Picasso than picture-perfect. "It's the cigarette you're worried about?"

Monique considered the moment and smiled. "I want you healthy when I lock you up."

He looked at her, dumbfounded, and smiled back. "You've got balls, I'll give you that!"

With both hands firmly on the steering wheel, he punched the gas again and the two of them disappeared into the lonely night.

On a deserted stretch of road, William and Monique sat in contemplative silence together, the soft glow of a petrol station visible a mile or two in the distance.

"Hell of a night," he said.

"Yes," she replied. "Hell of a night."

The gas station's lights, up ahead, grew nearer.

"Thank you for what you did back there," she said.

William looked at her and cracked a second, soft smile at her.

"I told you I'd fix it".

He really did like this woman. She was like him, a fighter and a winner. They would have made one Hell of a team together if circumstances were different.

"I need to freshen up and sort myself out. You need anything?" he asked her as they pulled into the Ruedi Rüssel gas station forecourt.

"No."

"Alright," he said, exiting the car, its engine still running as he entered the station's convenience store.

Once out of sight, he watched patiently through a side window as Monique Lefort exited the vehicle, ran towards the payphone at the side of the building, and dialed the emergency police number on the keypad.

"Smart move," he muttered under his breath, and with that, he made his way to the rear of the store, shouldered the back door, and stepped out into the pitch black.

His job was done. Now it was time to disappear, once and for all.

EPILOGUE

THE NEXT DAY, FROM THE COMFORT OF HER OWN IM-maculate and modernist apartment back in Paris, Monique Lefort was watching the local news channel. A female reporter was reporting live from Sinclair's residence in Switzerland.

"This is Pascale Lané reporting live from outside the Zürich residence of billionaire business tycoon Gabriel Sinclair who was found dead late last night in an apparent homicide."

Police cars swarmed the Zürich premises, ambulances and forensics teams filling the background.

Monique picked up the remote control to her television and switched it off. Nursing a crystal tumbler with a modest measure of V.S.O.P Cognac in it she sat, deep in thought, as a male police officer hovered in the background. A second female plainclothes officer sat at the table next to her writing her notes.

"I'll be finished here in a few minutes, Lieutenant."

"Yes, of course. Thank you," she responded politely. *Procedure was procedure after all.*

Monique's cell phone rang and she picked it up, puzzled by the withheld number.

"Oui. Hello?"

"It's me. I just wanted to make sure you're alright."

"I am."

"I'm sorry I had to bail on you back there. I had no choice."

"I know. Where are you?" she asked.

"Somewhere safe. Somewhere quiet."

Monique, seeking some privacy, got up from her chair and excused herself from the main room.

"Will I see you again?"

"I don't think so."

"You know I can't just let you go. You're a wanted criminal. I've got a job to do."

"I just wanted to make sure you were OK."

"I am, thank you."

"Then I'm happy—goodbye Monique, it's been a pleasure knowing you."

"You still owe me a new shirt or have you forgotten?" she added, waiting for his response.

William laughed. "No, I haven't forgotten. Not about you and not about your shirt. I'll get you something nice. Something special. I promise." With that, he hung up and the line went dead.

Monique held the phone to her lips, deep in thought. A thin trace of a smile on her face.

———————

BEHIND THE WHEEL OF A NEWLY STOLEN BMW, WILLIAM flipped shut the cell phone in his hand and tossed it on the seat beside him, a thin trace of a smile also on his face.

Out of the window, the road sign read BARCELONA - 176 km. *Time for some sun, sex, and sangria!* he thought to himself with a sly smirk.

With a sun-kissed landscape of sunflowers and cornfields on either side of him, he grabbed his pack of smokes, removed one and put it to his lips. Hesitating, and thinking back to what Monique had told him, he put his lighter down, replaced the cigarette, and then crushed the packet in his clenched fist. *I guess I'll take her advice after all* he told himself. *Should've given up years ago. Bloody disgusting habit.*

Cracking a broad smile, he cranked the volume and pumped the gas as the epic opening guitar riff to Muse's 'Supremacy' thumped through the surround sound speakers.

The engine roared as he chased the setting sun and cruised the Costa Brava coastline, carefree.

He'd done it. He'd won. He was back on top. Back where he belonged. He was winning!

Vacation my arse.

WTF WILL RETURN IN

ON THE
RUN

ABOUT THE AUTHOR

 Marc-Allen Barker was born in Paris, France, and was later raised and educated in Cheam, England. A competitive rugby player, he graduated from Epsom College with A-Levels in English Literature, French Classics, and Business Economics.

At the age of 18, he joined the French Army and enrolled with the 1st RHP Parachute Regiment in Tarbes. After successfully earning his wings and red beret, he served as a light weapons, communications, and field combat instructor for incoming recruits. On deployment with the United Nations in Bihac, Zagreb, and Sarajevo he carried out armed protection to humanitarian aid convoys - as well as reconnaissance and surveillance missions - during the Peace Talk process.

After graduating from Loughborough University with a BA in International Business he moved to Los Angeles, CA where he currently resides with his wife and son. In addition to world travel, Marc-Allen enjoys skydiving, scuba diving, and riding his motorcycles. Like William Trevor Francis, he also enjoys his Johnnie Walker Black Label 'rocks on the side'.

Made in United States
North Haven, CT
14 June 2025

69787464R00122